From Megan Maitland's Diary

Dear Diary,

Where to begin? So much has happened and my heart is so full. I'm finally allowed to proclaim to the world at large that Connor is my son, my own firstborn. Having him here with me is like an incredible Christmas gift to be unwrapped each and every morning!

I don't blame my father for what he did. An unmarried young girl with a baby was doomed to a terrible life back then. I'm so glad times have changed. And so very glad to discover that not only have I regained a son, but I've gained a grandson as well. My heart is filled to bursting! I even forgive the woman who perpetrated the hoax that would have only further separated me from Connor. After all, it didn't work, thank God.

It's been a very, very good year. It didn't seem so at the beginning, but it turned out far better than I could have ever dreamed. Which leads me to speculate about the year to come. Who knows what happiness is waiting just around the corner?

Dear Reader,

There's never a dull moment at Maitland Maternity! This unique and now world-renowned clinic was founded twenty-five years ago by Megan Maitland, widow of William Maitland, of the prominent Austin, Texas, Maitlands. Megan is also matriarch of an impressive family of seven children, many of whom are active participants in the everyday miracles that bring children into the world.

When our series began, the family was stunned by the unexpected arrival of an unidentified baby at the clinic— unidentified, except for the claim that the child is a ` Maitland. Who are the parents of this child? Is the claim legitimate? Will the media's tenacious grip on this news damage the clinic's reputation? Suddenly, rumors and counterclaims abound. Women claiming to be the child's mother materialize out of the woodwork! How will Megan get at the truth? And how will the media circus affect the lives and loves of the Maitland children—Abby, the head of gynecology, Ellie, the hospital administrator, her twin sister, Beth, who runs the day care center, Mitchell, the fertility specialist, R.J., the vice president of operations— even Anna, who has nothing to do with the clinic, and Jake, the black sheep of the family?

We're thrilled to bring you the long-awaited culmination to Connor Maitland's story and to offer the solution to the mystery of the Maitland baby in *A Dad at Last!*

Marsha Zinberg,
Senior Editor and Editorial Co-ordinator, Special Projects

MARIE FERRARELLA

A Dad at Last

Published by Silhouette Books
America's Publisher of Contemporary Romance

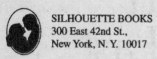

SILHOUETTE BOOKS
300 East 42nd St.,
New York, N. Y. 10017

ISBN 0-373-65073-6

A DAD AT LAST

Copyright © 2000 by Enterprises S.A.

Marie Ferrarella is acknowledged as the author of this work.

This edition published by arrangement with Harlequin Books S.A.

® and TM are trademarks of Harlequin Books S.A., used under license. Trademarks indicated with ® are registered in the United States Patent and Trademark Office, the Canadian Trade Marks Office and in other countries.

Visit Silhouette at www.eHarlequin.com

Printed in U.S.A.

Prolific romance author **Marie Ferrarella** claims, "I was born writing, which must have made the delivery especially difficult for my mother!" Born in West Germany of Polish parents, she came to America when she was four years of age. For an entire year, Marie and her family explored the eastern half of the country before finally settling in New York. It was there, at the age of fourteen, that she met the man she would marry, her first true love, Charles Ferrarella.

During her days at Queens College, acting started to lose its glamour as Marie spent more and more time writing. After receiving her English degree, specializing in Shakespearean comedy, Marie and her family moved to Southern California, where she still resides today. After an interminable seven weeks apart, Charles decided he couldn't live without her, and came out to California to marry his childhood sweetheart. Marie, who has written over one hundred novels, wrote both the introduction and conclusion to Connor Maitland's miraculous reunion with his family and was delighted to participate in the Maitland family saga. She keeps her fingers crossed that her many fans enjoy reading her books as much as she enjoys writing them.

To Marsha Zinberg,
with thanks for a great time.

PROLOGUE

THE MOONLIGHT surrounded Connor O'Hara like a cold shroud as he picked his way slowly beside the isolated train tracks.

Funny how things turned out sometimes.

He'd only just found out he had a son, and now that little boy's life depended on a group of men he hadn't met until a few months ago. Men who were at this moment laying their own lives on the line, shielded only by the inky cloak of night and their bravery as they crept toward the abandoned sugar factory ahead, where he'd been told to meet Chase's kidnappers.

It was asking a lot, yet they had volunteered without a single word from him.

The door to the sugar factory opened. A small ball of light, thanks to a lantern, illuminated the players for Connor.

Janelle Davis, the epitome of confidence, sauntered ahead of the man who accompanied her. In her arms was Connor's son.

Even in the poor light, Connor could see her eyes

glinting as they washed over him. She fairly glowed with triumph.

The humor that twisted her mouth was cynical. "So you came. I knew you would." She glanced at the child in her arms. "For the brat."

Connor had never felt hatred like this before. It clogged his throat like thick bile, almost choking him. His eyes narrowed as he looked at the woman who'd stolen his child and done heaven only knew what else. She was standing beside the tall, rugged-looking man who'd been impersonating Connor for the past few months. Petey gave no indication of being the puppet she had, with her wiles, forced him to be.

Hatred mingled with fear, fear for the child she held in her arms, the child Connor knew she could, without compunction, kill in an instant. Destroying Chase as if he were nothing more than a rag doll, a prop to further her goal.

He stalled for time. Positions had to be reached. A single word emerged from his lips as his eyes nailed her where she stood.

"Why?"

Janelle shrugged a slim, careless shoulder. Her eyes told him she was enjoying this a great deal. She liked having the upper hand.

"Not all of us are born rich." The smile turned cruel. "A girl's gotta look out for herself."

Her hold on the baby tightened, and her eyes slid

to the suitcase Connor held in his hand as Chase whimpered. "You have the money?"

He raised the case. "Right here."

Her sharp eyes looked around. There were no cars in the area save the one Connor had parked in the distance. Just the way she'd told him. "And you're alone."

His expression never changed. Neither did the loathing he knew was in his eyes. "Those were your instructions."

She laughed shortly, toying with him, ignoring her husband Petey's growing agitation. "Too bad you couldn't have stayed back at your ranch, Connor. Would have saved us both a lot of time and grief." The smile vanished. She was all business. "Take the suitcase, Petey."

But Connor held the case back as Petey reached for it. "Give me my son."

"Paternal affection. How touching," she mocked. "Maybe we should have asked for more than five million, Petey. Looks like the daddy of the year would have been willing to fork it over."

Connor knew he had to get Chase away from Janelle. The plan couldn't go forward as long as the baby was in danger.

Tired, anxious, Petey looked at his wife. What was she trying to do? They had what they came for within their reach. Why was she playing games? "Damn it, Janelle, just give him the kid."

The exasperated look on her face cut him dead. It told him what a fool she thought he was. "Take the case first, you idiot."

Connor handed the suitcase to Petey.

Eagerness replaced anger. Petey dropped to the ground, placing the suitcase before him. Hands shaking, he opened it. Cross words were forgotten as he looked over his shoulder at Janelle. "It's here. You were right. It's all here."

Janelle stepped forward to see for herself. The suitcase was filled with neat stacks of carefully bound bills, all facing in the same direction. "We won't know if it's all there until we count it."

"It's all there," Connor told her through tight lips. "I wouldn't endanger the life of my son."

Her expression was smug. "No, you wouldn't. All right, close the case and get on your feet, Petey." He did as she ordered. "Aim the gun at his belly. Anything goes wrong, shoot him and then the baby."

With a mocking smile on her lips, she handed Connor his son.

Taking Chase into his arms, he had no time to wonder at this newfound fatherhood or unwrap and examine any of the emotions that were sweeping over him as he felt the weight of his son in his arms for the very first time.

It was now or never.

Moving swiftly, Connor pushed Janelle out of his

way and ducked into the protective shelter of the sugar factory.

In the background, the sound of shouting was followed by a single exchange of gunfire.

CHAPTER ONE

"IF YOU KNOT those fingers together any tighter, we're going to have to call in one of the doctors from the hospital to surgically untangle them."

Startled, lost in her thoughts, Lacy Clark looked up to see Megan Maitland standing beside her in the living room, smiling compassionately at her. She hadn't heard the older woman approach.

Self-consciously, Lacy realized that she'd been knotting and unknotting her hands, an outward sign of the inner turmoil that had been going on for what seemed like half an eternity. Ever since Connor and the others had left to meet the kidnappers.

She'd pleaded to go with them so she could see what was happening firsthand instead of having her imagination run riot. But Connor had insisted that having her there would put them all at risk, so she'd agreed to stay behind, dying a little more with each tick of the grandfather clock in the hall.

"Sorry," she murmured.

Lacy dropped her hands to her sides. Her fingers might no longer be tangled, but that didn't relieve the knot in her stomach. She couldn't stand being in the dark like this anymore. She'd been in the dark for so long now, about so many things, this added uncertainty was almost intolerable.

Where were they? Where was her son?

Pressing her lips together, she looked toward the door. Her whole world was out there somewhere, beyond her reach. Beyond her ability to do anything about it. Somewhere, lost in the night, was the baby who had been missing from her life these past eleven months while she'd wandered through a haze of amnesia, thanks to Janelle. The baby who could very well continue to be missing forever if Connor and the others didn't succeed with their plan.

What would she do if she never saw Chase again? Her heart felt as if it was twisting around in her chest.

"You've nothing to be sorry about." Megan gave Lacy's hand a warm squeeze, knowing what the young mother must be going through. "They'll bring him back to you, I promise."

They'd set up vigil here in the Maitland house, Megan, her daughter Abby, her daughter-in-law Camille, Shelby Lord and Lacy, to wait for the men who had gone to retrieve that one small, lost child and bring him safely back.

To bring back the grandson Megan hadn't found a way to acknowledge yet. Not without upsetting life as everyone here knew it. A life that had already suffered so many storms, so many onslaughts these last few months. It seemed almost more than one family could endure.

But they would. That was what made them strong and made them Maitlands.

"And if that scum manages to escape somehow," Abby said to Lacy as she came up on her other side, "there isn't a rock in this state big enough for Janelle and Petey to crawl under. We'll find them, Lacy. I promise." She added her vow to her mother's.

Shelby joined the tight group, her indignation at the kidnapping riding another fresh wave. Both her brothers, Michael and Garrett, were with Connor tonight. She laid one hand on Lacy's shoulder and one on Abby's. "Hell, with our combined resources and efforts, we could find a red ant in a mile-wide strawberry patch. One bitch, her henchman and a baby shouldn't be any problem."

"We're getting ahead of ourselves," Camille softly warned them. She looked at Lacy. "There isn't any reason to believe that Jake, Connor and the others *haven't* been successful."

Lacy knew what they were trying to do and she was grateful to all of them. But it still didn't quell the uneasiness she felt. The uneasiness that continued to grow.

"If they've been successful, why haven't they called?" She heard herself demanding.

Strong, terse, the voice hardly seemed to belong

to her. But she'd been through a great deal these past few months.

This last year and then some, she amended mentally. She'd had Connor's baby in secret, only to be forced to leave him on the doorstep of Maitland Maternity Clinic for his own good. And she'd lost eleven months out of her life when Janelle had assaulted her in that alley behind the hospital, leaving her for dead. Leaving her to wander through the misty, cottony world of amnesia when she came to, with no knowledge of herself or the child she'd left unguarded.

Lacy looked accusingly at the silent telephone on the coffee table. "Why isn't the phone ringing right now?" It didn't seem like an unreasonable request. "There're five of them. One of them's got to have a cell phone—or change for a public phone." She knew the answer to her own question. "They're not calling because something went wrong."

Watching Lacy, sharing her agony, Megan felt her heart contract.

She'd been like that once, Megan thought. Forty-six years ago, pregnant, unmarried and deserted by her baby's father, she'd been just like Lacy. Scared, frightened and not knowing where to turn. So she had turned inward and somehow found the will to go on. Like Lacy, she would have kept her baby once he was born. But unlike Lacy, someone she'd trusted with all her heart had taken her baby from her at the moment of birth and lied to her. A lie that would come back to haunt her.

Her father had told her that the son she'd had as a result of a young, impetuous romantic interlude with Clyde Mitchum had been stillborn. After she'd cried an ocean of tears, she'd pulled herself together and found the strength to continue. Not just continue but eventually win the heart of William Maitland and, with him, forge a dynasty of her own.

Now that wonderful family she and her late husband had created were there to offer their support to her whenever she needed them.

Megan couldn't help wondering how far that support could be stretched. Once they knew Connor was not her long-estranged nephew but rather her long-lost son, would that support break down? Or would it rally and grow stronger still for the adversity the situation represented?

She could only pray for the latter. One way or another, she would have her answer soon enough.

But right now, it was her grandson she was concerned about. Her grandson who had to be rescued and brought back to the fold. The details and explanations could be handled later. First things first.

She slipped an arm around Lacy's thin shoulders, feeling as if, in a way, she was somehow stepping into the past and comforting herself.

"There are dozens of reasons they haven't called, Lacy, and none of them are bad." A slight smile curved her lips. "And no matter what the television commercials would have us believe, not everyone carries around a cell phone in their hip pocket."

"And even if they did," Shelby interjected, "it doesn't necessarily mean it's working. Garrett can't remember to charge the one I gave him to save his life. Says it's a nuisance."

Lacy sighed, praying they were right. That it was just a matter of not taking the time or finding the opportunity to call. Maybe they were, even now, on their way home. Home with her son.

But she couldn't calm down.

The agitation was growing steadily, threatening to consume her. "Well, right now it's a nuisance I really wish he'd put up with." She could only hope that didn't come out as short as it sounded. Lacy knew that Connor didn't own a cell phone, but that shouldn't have prevented him from finding a way to call.

She looked at the telephone again, willing it to ring. It remained silent.

He wasn't calling because something horrible had happened. She just knew it.

Unable to remain still, she began to pace again, her eyes all but riveted to the front door with every step she took. Why weren't they back yet? The meeting was for midnight. It was past two.

Unable to remain on the sidelines any longer, Shelby checked her pockets for her car keys.

"Maybe I'll just take a ride up to the sugar factory to see if everything went the way it should have."

Megan instinctively took a step to block her way. "No." It was an order. "It's too dangerous."

Shelby looked at the Maitland family matriarch. Years ago Megan had taken Shelby and her brothers and sister under her wing when their own parents had abandoned them. Though she had arranged for the children to be adopted by friends of hers, Megan had always been like an aunt—or at times a second mother—to the Lord children. Shelby realized there was no point arguing, but she wasn't happy about doing nothing.

Sensing the struggle she'd created within the younger woman, Megan mitigated her words with logic. "Besides, they might be on their way home already, and you'll wind up missing them. No sense in driving up there for no reason. Better to stay put."

"All right." Shelby relented, slipping her keys into her pocket. "I'll give them another half an hour, but after that I'm out of here." As if to back up her position, she took out her cell phone and held it up for inspection. "And I've got a fully charged cell phone, so if they do show up while I'm gone, you can reach me the minute they walk in."

"I'll go with you," Lacy told her. Megan opened her mouth to protest, but Lacy wasn't about to be talked out of it. "I can't take this waiting any longer,

Mrs. Maitland, and if I pace anymore, you're going to have a path worn through your tile.''

Megan shrugged carelessly. As if that mattered. "I was getting tired of that pattern anyway," she quipped. "And I know how you feel." Her eyes held the younger woman's. She saw doubt. "I really do.''

There was something in the older woman's eyes that spoke to her, though for the life of her, Lacy didn't understand how Megan Maitland could have the vaguest idea what it was like to be an unwed mother whose child had been kidnapped. Megan, who together with her husband had founded the prestigious Maitland Maternity Clinic, where the country's rich and famous came to have their babies, rubbing shoulders with desperate young women who had their backs up against the wall and nowhere to turn—women for whom the clinic had originally been created. But Megan Maitland was far removed from the world Lacy knew. She could easily buy and sell half the people in Austin without blinking an eye. How could she possibly know what it was like to be so destitute that she had nowhere to turn?

But she did have somewhere to turn, Lacy reminded herself. She had a job as a chef at Austin Eats Diner. Shelby Lord had taken her in and given her that job when she had amnesia. After a blow to the head had restored her memory, Shelby said nothing had changed. The job was hers for as long as she wanted it.

So she had a job and friends now, friends who had been eager to help reunite her with her baby. Friends who were willing to risk themselves and the ones they loved to do it. She might not have money like Megan, but she was rich in her own way. Rich in friends.

Lacy smiled. Maybe she had more in common with Megan than she'd thought.

"Wait." Shelby held up a hand to stop the other women from talking. "Table the talk about driving over to the sugar factory, I think I hear a car. Two cars," she amended.

Lacy was at the front door before Shelby finished speaking, pulling it open in time to see the two cars that had driven up and turned off their headlights.

"They're back," she cried, running out to meet them, her heart hammering wildly.

"Wait, Lacy," Megan called.

Her back to the house, Lacy didn't hear her. She didn't hear or see anything but the tall man coming toward her.

Moonlight outlined his long frame and the tan Stetson he wore. In the dark it was difficult at first to see that he was holding something in his arms. Or what that something was.

Her mother's heart told her even before her eyes could adjust.

Lacy didn't remember crossing the last five feet to Connor. Didn't remember her feet hitting the ground in a dead run. All she was aware of was that her eyes had filled with tears, making it difficult to focus.

She could have made her way to her son's side blindfolded.

Lacy clutched Connor's arm, looking into the face of her sleeping son.

"You found him," she sobbed. "And he's so big."

The baby she remembered holding to her breast had been almost a newborn, certainly not this thriving child with his fair hair and rounded face.

As if in response to her voice, Chase opened his eyes, looking at her with wonder. A sweet smile moved the small, rosebud mouth.

Something warm opened up smack in the middle of Connor's chest. He had trouble dealing with it. "He knows you," Connor said.

Lacy wanted to say yes, even though she knew it was almost too much to hope for. She and Chase had been apart for so many months. Important months. But for the moment, she told herself that it was true.

"He had a very sweet disposition," she murmured, taking her son into her arms.

It felt like heaven.

She hadn't realized until this very second how much her arms had ached for this small weight. How much her heart had ached to feel the baby's heart beating next to hers.

Happiness threatened to overwhelm her. It was almost more than she could humanly stand.

"Oh, thank you," she murmured, raising her eyes to Connor and the men who were gathered behind him. "Thank you all for bringing my baby back to me."

"Can we hold the thanks until we get into the house?" Garrett Lord requested. The month-old wound in his shoulder still ached, and he needed a painkiller.

Belatedly, Connor realized that Lacy had rushed out in her bare feet. Sometimes the woman didn't have the sense she was born with. She could hurt herself on the stony drive.

"Get inside before we add a sprained ankle to the list of things that've gone wrong for you," he ordered, slipping an arm around her.

Some things might have gone wrong, Lacy thought, but other things had gone very right. She had her baby back, and Connor, however temporarily, was in her life once more. There was no way she felt in the wrong tonight.

"Throw away the list," Lacy told him. Without being conscious of it, she leaned into Connor as they walked to the house, absorbing the strength that radiated from him. "All that matters is that you found Chase and brought him back to me."

"Not quite all," Jake Maitland corrected, coming in behind them. He shrugged out of his jacket and tossed it onto the coatrack, snaring a hook. He wrapped one arm around his wife's waist and pulled her toward him, pausing to kiss Camille before he continued. He noted that the women were all looking at him, waiting for him to continue. "I think equally important is that Janelle is finally behind bars, and if there's any justice in this world, will never bother you or anyone else in this family—" he looked at his mother "—again."

"What about Connor?" Abby asked, then immediately realized her mistake. "I mean Petey."

"Well, he's not going to be sharing a cell with Janelle, that's for damn sure," Michael told her.

Megan turned from Michael and looked at her youngest son's face for confirmation. Jake grimly nodded. "He had a gun with him. When we showed up, Janelle goaded him into shooting it out with us instead of giving up. Petey didn't stand a chance."

"Petey?" Lacy echoed. She looked at Connor. "Was that his name?"

Connor nodded. "That was his name. Seems he was married to Janelle, the poor bastard." He shrugged. "Maybe he's better off this way. No telling what she had up her sleeve for him next. That woman had him jumping through flaming hoops and swearing it was his idea." He saw the quizzical look in Lacy's eyes. "He talked a little before he died. What he didn't tell us, Janelle did."

Once she'd stopped cursing them all to hell, she'd

made an about-face and confessed. Proudly. It left Connor mystified how the woman could be so proud of being so evil and spreading that poison into so many lives.

Megan shook her head. It all seemed like such a horrible waste to her. Greed and jealousy were terrible things. She cleared her throat, glad to be done with this chapter.

"The important thing is that it's all over." Megan's eyes swept the young men and women in her home, her gratitude evident. For the first time in days, she felt like eating. "What do you say we all go into the kitchen and I'll see if I can fix us a celebratory late dinner." She thought of the time. It was close to dawn. "Or early breakfast, as it were," she amended. "All this tension has helped me work up an appetite."

Assenting murmurs went up, but Megan noticed that Connor began to distance himself from the others. Their eyes met, and she raised a silent brow.

"If it's all the same to you, I'd just as soon go up to my room and get some sleep right now," he said. "I'm about ready to drop in my tracks."

Megan felt a smattering of disappointment. Now that this major hurdle had been resolved to their satisfaction, she would have thought that Connor would want to remain with his son and his son's mother, at least for a little while.

But she was well versed in reading expressions.

One look at him told her not to push. Connor had his reasons for withdrawing. Maybe he needed a little time to assimilate all that had happened. From what she gathered, he hadn't even known he had a son until just after the kidnapping had come to light and Lacy had regained her memory.

"Of course, Connor," she agreed. "You must be exhausted."

Maybe it was better if they all went to bed for what was left of the night. That way, they'd be fresh when she dropped her bombshell—and prayed for the best. Besides, the rest of her children needed to be here. She wasn't about to go through that emotion-wrenching announcement more than once. It needed to be made to everyone at the same time. She felt bad enough that Ellie had accidentally overheard and had borne the weight of knowing her secret alone.

Megan had made up her mind. From now on, no more secrets of any kind, no matter how innocent.

"You all have to be exhausted," she acknowledged, looking at the others. "Why don't we postpone any sort of celebration until I can do this up properly?" Her eyes swept over Connor first, then touched everyone in the room one by one until they came to rest on Lacy. The mother of her grandchild.

"Sounds good to me," Jake murmured. He slung his arm around Camille, his eyes drooping just a shade. "Care to prop up a hero? Help me up to bed and I'll give you all the details, bit by bit."

Before Camille could comment, Abby's beeper went off, pulsing red numbers. Angling it away from her belt, Abby made out the telephone number. It was only vaguely familiar. She made a guess.

"Probably Mrs. Marlow. She looked ready to pop when I saw her in the office yesterday. Twins this time." Two cups of coffee should give her a second wind, she estimated, sighing. "Another post-midnight delivery. Perfect ending to a perfect day." On her way to the den and the telephone, Abby stopped long enough to brush a kiss on Connor's cheek. "Nice work, cousin. Looks like you found the family just in time."

He wasn't sure if she was referring to the fact that, in being reunited with the Maitlands, he was able to get the help he needed to recover his son or if there was something else behind her words. All he did know was that the term she'd applied to him was incorrect.

He wasn't her cousin, he was her half brother.

It was on the tip of his tongue to say something. But it wasn't up to him to make the correction, he reminded himself. The words, whatever she ultimately chose them to be, belonged to Megan. He knew the circumstances surrounding his birth and his subsequent secretive adoption. He'd only learned them recently himself. Connor couldn't even imagine what Megan must have gone through, thinking him dead all these years, only to have him turn up now, not her nephew, as she'd believed, but her son. Had to be a lot to deal with. He owed it to her to be the one to let the others know.

Or keep the secret to herself.

He had a lot to deal with himself, he thought, finding out he had a child of his own he hadn't known about. He supposed in a way that gave him something in common with his birth mother.

It was going to be hard, making the transition. Thinking of Megan Maitland as his mother instead of Clarise O'Hara, the woman who had raised him. The mother he'd buried almost two years ago.

Reaching the foot of the stairs, Connor glanced toward Lacy. Part of him was tempted to remain with her. To say things to her that had occurred to him both before and after he and the others had rescued Chase. But he didn't want to be hasty. There was a wealth of feelings churning inside him, feelings that had to be sorted out and examined before he did anything about them.

He had learned a long time ago not to say things in the heat of the moment or when he was too exhausted to think clearly. Anything worth saying would keep until morning, when he was more lucid and had the time to think things through. He didn't want to say things to Lacy he'd only have to take back later, no matter how much he suddenly wanted to say them. She'd been through enough without having him add to her grief.

"Night," he murmured, nodding at Shelby and her brothers, who were on their way out the door, then at Lacy and Megan. "I'll see you in the morning."

Lacy tightened her arms around her son, watching the only man she'd ever cared about, the only man she'd fallen in love with—not once, but twice—disappear up the stairs.

Squaring her shoulders, she turned to Megan. "I guess maybe I'd better be leaving, too."

Megan shook her head. "You'll do no such thing. You're in no condition to drive anywhere tonight. Look at you—you're flushed and your eyes look like they're liable to close any minute. All we need now is to have you fall asleep at the wheel and drive into some ditch. You're staying here tonight. The nursery's still there for Chase, and you're welcome to your pick of bedrooms."

"I wouldn't argue with her if I were you," Abby advised Lacy with an affectionate wink. "No one's ever won."

Lacy smiled her gratitude. She *was* exhausted. "Then I guess I'm staying the night."

Megan patted her arm. "Smart girl. Now let's go and get you settled in."

Though she liked the independence she had so recently embraced, it was nice, Lacy thought as she followed Megan up the stairs, being taken care of just this once.

CHAPTER TWO

CONNOR FELT like hell.

He probably looked it, too, he surmised, making his way down the back stairs. It was early, and the others, he assumed, were still asleep. Just as well. He preferred it that way. Fewer people to interact with. He wasn't exactly at his social best at the moment.

He hadn't gotten more than a thimbleful of sleep before he'd given up and gotten out of bed. There was so much on his mind, so many emotions running rampant through him, demanding to be addressed, that when his body had finally surrendered to exhaustion, the sleep that had come to him had been fitful, leaving Connor more tired, if possible, when he awoke than when he'd finally fallen asleep.

He was no fresher this morning than he had been hours before. And therefore, he concluded, he was in no better condition to make decisions now than then. Worse, if he were being honest.

So when he stumbled down the stairs, led by instinct to the kitchen and, he hoped, mud-strong coffee set on a timer, and came across Lacy and Chase instead, the reaction that suddenly came over him was not one he fully trusted. Likely, it had more to do with his physical state than his emotional one.

But it was the emotional one that was responding.

A feeling of awe and something Connor couldn't quite put a name to filled him, pushing its way to every corner of his being like late morning sunshine seeking to chase out the last remnants of the night's shadows.

Lacy, her back to him, was feeding the baby. Connor leaned his shoulder against the doorjamb and quietly watched this tiny, shining moment of motherhood in action.

He'd always kept his own counsel, playing everything so close to the chest, it was almost completely undetected by the average person who passed through his life. No one could ever have accused Connor of being an emotional man. He had always believed that emotions got in the way of things. To give in to them undermined your stamina, your resolve. The way to face life was stoically, shouldering responsibilities that came along and moving ahead one day at a time. If that sort of philosophy made the road lonely, at least the terrain was negotiable. And, ultimately, that was the most important thing.

But this, whatever "this" was, didn't fit into his way of life. This feeling didn't even have a name, at least not one he was willing to affix to it. But it had breadth and texture and substance nonetheless, looming suddenly rather large in his world.

And it had to do not only with the small being who had come into his life less than twelve hours ago, but with Lacy, as well.

Connor straightened, trying desperately to straighten his thinking, as well. This thing he was struggling with was just responsibility under a different guise, nothing more, he told himself. That was what was nagging at him, defying definition. Just an overwhelming sense of responsibility.

After all, he'd never been a father before. Fatherhood brought with it a wealth of obligations. Not the least of which was an obligation to the child's mother.

Lacy.

He knew he had to do the right thing, by her and by the child. It was wrestling with what exactly the right thing was that was troubling him.

And no wonder. He was forty-five years old, a hell of a time to have his world upended and find himself a father for the first time.

Damn, a revelation like that, especially without warning, would have thrown a bigger man than him off, Connor reasoned.

Lacy didn't bother looking over her shoulder. Instead, she finally asked, ''Are you going to hover by the doorway all morning, or are you going to come in and take a look at your son in the daylight?''

Feeling slightly foolish, like a man caught where

he shouldn't be, Connor cleared his throat as he walked into the kitchen. "You knew I was there?"

Her mouth curved. She'd sensed his presence even before Connor had reached the bottom of the stairs.

Funny how someone who had been such a huge part of her life once had vanished from her mind for those long, lonely months she'd spent groping for her lost memory. Lacy would have sworn that nothing would have been able to erase Connor O'Hara from her thoughts. Maybe he wasn't as indelibly imprinted there as she'd once believed. She hadn't even recognized him when he'd first come into the diner.

As she looked back now, that astounded her, amnesia or no amnesia. So much of her heart had been and still was tangled up with Connor.

It always would be, she thought, now that she had Chase.

Spooning some more cereal past her son's very messy lips, she smiled. This felt so right. She blessed all the books on early child rearing she'd devoured once she knew of her condition. At least there would be no awkwardness with her son the way there was with his father.

She glanced over her shoulder at Connor. He looked as if he hadn't slept. Was that because of her? Or was it just because of everything that had happened last night?

She told herself not to nurse any false hopes. She'd been that route before and been sorely disappointed.

"You're not exactly invisible, you know. Why didn't you just come into the kitchen? There's certainly room enough."

There was room enough in the kitchen for a minor convention. Megan—his mother, he amended—liked it that way, he'd heard. Enough room for everyone in the family to gather and bring a friend if they felt like it. Megan considered the kitchen the heart of the house. As if such things were possible, he thought, dismissing the notion as foolish.

Connor shrugged. "You seemed busy with Chase, and I didn't want to interrupt."

Letting Chase feed himself a finger of toast, she turned to look at Connor squarely. God, but she did love this man, no matter what. She knew she always would. But that was her problem, not his.

"You're not," she told him briskly, then softened. He did look like thirty miles of bad road, but even so, he was as handsome as they came. "He's yours as well as mine. He wouldn't be here right now if not for you—twice over," she added, her mouth curving in a whimsical smile.

Last night had been a team effort. There was no way he could have gotten Chase away safely if not for Jake, Michael and Garrett.

"I didn't do that much. The others— Oh." The full impact of her words finally hit him. She meant fathering Chase. "Yes, well…"

His voice trailed off, led away by fragments of

memory that drifted in then faded again, incomplete. He paused, grappling with questions, with things that needed clearing up.

The time, he decided, was probably never going to be more right than now. If he didn't ask, the opportunity would only drift further and further away from him.

He moved so that he was beside her and could see her face when she spoke.

Connor shoved his hands into his jeans. "Why didn't you tell me?" She raised her eyes to look at him. "About Chase. Why didn't you tell me you were pregnant when you found out, and that the baby you were carrying was mine?" Against his will, he remembered the single night they'd shared. How soft, how delicate she'd felt in his arms. Like a dream that had descended to earth for the duration of dusk to dawn.

Her hand tightening on the spoon, Lacy unconsciously raised her chin. She pretended to be completely engrossed in feeding Chase, coaxing another spoonful of food between his lips. "I didn't want you to think I wanted anything from you."

"I could have helped you with the bills—"

Her face clouded. Didn't he understand what she was saying? It wasn't his money she'd wanted or needed. It was his love. And that she couldn't have, so the rest never mattered.

"I didn't want that."

He pulled a chair around, straddling it so that he faced her. She wasn't making any sense. "Yet you left the baby on the steps of the hospital because you couldn't take care of him."

She flinched at the accusation in his voice. It was something she'd berated herself for a hundred times over.

"I'll never forgive myself for that." Her voice was solemn, hollow. "But it was one unpardonable moment of weakness, because Janelle was after me and I was afraid she'd hurt the baby." She bit her lip. She'd been desperate, with nowhere to turn, her back to the wall. "Still, there was no excuse for doing it that way."

Frustrated, he dragged his hand through his hair. That wasn't the point. The torment in her eyes sparked his guilt. Damn it, it wasn't his intention to make her blame herself. "I didn't mean—God knows you paid for that."

"Not enough." Lacy blinked back tears that had suddenly risen to her eyes. She could have lost Chase forever. She looked at the face of her son. The wide, happy grin was smeared with custard-colored cereal. With the edge of his bib, she wiped the stains away. "I'm going to spend the rest of my life making it up to him—if I can."

Damn it, why wasn't this coming out right? He wasn't trying to accuse her of anything, just trying to get to the bottom of her reasoning, or what passed for it. "Aren't you being a little hard on yourself?"

But she shook her head, refusing to accept absolution. "If something had happened to him, I couldn't be hard enough to make up for that—"

He sighed. They were veering off track. "Lacy— I had a right to know."

Her eyes met his for a moment before she began feeding Chase again.

"Yes, you did," she replied quietly. "I know that now and I'm sorry I didn't tell you. But I didn't want to spring a baby on you, not after what you'd told me. If you recall, at the time you said things like we weren't right for each other and that I deserved someone who could give me a family. Something you made quite clear you weren't willing to do. That's why I believed that letter Janelle gave me, claiming you wrote it. The one that gave me the brush-off."

"This isn't about Janelle. She duped both of us, not to mention the family and she's going to be made to pay for everything she's done. I wouldn't have left you a note, but in a way…"

"In a way?" She prodded him, feeling the heat of anger rising within her.

This wasn't coming out right. Talking wasn't his long suit. He was just thinking of Lacy. "Forty-five's a little old to start all over again."

Age was just a number to her. Other factors meant so much more. "Only if you want it to be. Twenty-five's old if the circumstances arrange themselves that way.''

She was trying not to let her temper get the best of her, but it was becoming very hard not to give in. Connor had deliberately turned his back on something wonderful because of a number.

''The trick is not to let it be. The real trick is to want something so much that age or any other obstacle has nothing to do with it and isn't allowed to get in your way.'' She shrugged, telling herself it didn't matter. Knowing she was lying. ''You didn't want any of this.''

What he'd professed he'd wanted had no bearing on what was now a reality. ''Still, it—he,'' Connor amended, annoyed with himself at the slip, ''is here and I have a responsibility—''

Responsibility. It took everything she had not to scream. ''God, you couldn't have come up with a colder word if you tried, do you know that?''

Women were creatures Connor knew he just couldn't begin to fathom. He was better off with horses. At least there were manuals about dealing with horses. ''What cold word? What are you talking about? The father of a child has certain responsibilities to that child—''

Lacy fought tears. He didn't have the vaguest idea what it took to be a father. What hurt was that he didn't realize it. There was no point in getting angry, she thought. What was involved was beyond his comprehension.

"Not any you'd understand," she said dully.

She was rambling again. He caught her hand as she was about to give Chase the last bit of the cereal. "What?"

Her eyes on his, she waited him out. He released her hand. "You're talking money, aren't you?"

Exasperation threatened to undo the calm exterior he was trying to maintain for the sake of the baby. "Yes, I'm talking money."

She started to say something, then thought better of it. It was like trying to explain the nuances of a piano keyboard to a man who was utterly tone-deaf. "No, thank you."

She was a little too quick to turn her back on his offer. It galled him.

"And just how do you intend to pay for his food? His clothing? His education when the time comes?" Connor demanded, his voice rising. "The tooth fairy isn't going to magically make it happen. Only money takes care of things like that—and I have money."

And apparently nothing else, Lacy thought. She looked at him, sorrow deep in her eyes.

He didn't know whether to be insulted or not. He settled for annoyed. "What?"

Lacy pressed her lips together, shaking her head slightly. "Nothing. It's just that for a little while back there, when I saw you walking from the car with our son in your arms, I thought you had something else to offer.''

More fool she was for thinking so, she upbraided herself. When was she going to learn that she'd had a happier outcome than most? Her baby was alive and well and so was she. That was the most she could hope for. Happy endings only existed in fairy tales, and Connor had made it very clear what he thought of things like that.

He blew out an angry breath. ''Can't barter with 'something else.''' Connor wanted her to see reason. Was that too much to ask? ''Money is what counts in this world.''

An iciness slipped over her heart. Had she been so blind? So wrong about the man Connor O'Hara really was? ''Do you really believe that?''

''Yes.'' He wasn't a slave to money and it wasn't his god, but he knew what the world was like, what happened to people who couldn't pay. They did without and grew bitter in the end. Look what the desire for money had driven Janelle to do.

If he only knew how much it hurt to hear him say things like that, Lacy thought. She'd been right to leave his ranch when she found out she was pregnant. There was no love in Connor's heart, no compassion. And those values she wanted passed on to her son.

Very quietly, she slipped the spoon into the bowl, then wiped the last of his breakfast from Chase's face. "Then I guess there's not much difference between you and Janelle, is there?"

Now what was she talking about? He swore silently, feeling he couldn't follow the conversation without a road map. Here he was, trying to make sure that Chase and she were provided for, and she was behaving as if he was trying to have her stoned in the town square as an undesirable. "I wouldn't try to steal it."

"No, you wouldn't. You're much too honorable for that." And that was just the problem. She didn't want him being honorable, she wanted him being passionate, being moved that he had living, flesh-and-blood proof that he existed, that he could love.

She supposed she was being naive again. Just like the last time.

Connor resented the way she twisted what he was trying to say and do. "Why do you make *honorable* sound as if it's a dirty word?"

Megan picked that moment to sweep into the kitchen, curtailing the conversation.

Drawn by the sound of Connor's and Lacy's raised voices, she'd debated turning and leaving, then had decided against it. The two had been through a great deal, both separately and together. By all rights, their emotions probably bore an acute resemblance to Swiss cheese by now. What they needed as they stood there swiping at each other was not a referee, but time out. Time to heal.

She intended to give it to them.

"Hello, I thought I'd find you here," she said to Lacy. "But not you." That had been for Connor. Looking from one to the other, she deliberately kept her expression blank. "Am I interrupting something?"

"No," Connor growled, turning away from them toward the counter. A coffee urn, filled to the brim, stood to the side, all but forgotten in the heat of the moment. "I just came down for coffee."

"Me, too," Megan told him cheerfully, determined to keep the peace. She took three cups and saucers out of the cupboard, lining them up on the counter. "Can't seem to begin my day without at least two cups." Pressing the spigot, she filled the first cup to the rim. "Used to be one, but the body slows down with age." Megan sighed appropriately, then smiled at her firstborn. "Although I'm determined to fight it all the way."

She set down the first cup and filled the second, glancing over her shoulder at Chase as she did so. Even the tiny scrap of a look caused her heart to tighten. She dearly loved the little boy. In a small way, having him with her these past months made up for missing out on Connor's first year.

"I missed looking in on him during the night."

There was nothing but everlasting gratitude in Lacy's heart toward Megan Maitland. "I didn't get a chance to tell you how much I appreciate everything you've done for Chase.''

Megan waved away the words, embarrassed. "No need to thank me, especially since he's family.'' The birthmark crescent on Chase's tummy had been proof enough for Megan. It was reminiscent of the one that had been in the same area on Connor's father. Although birthmarks weren't necessarily inherited, this one was too unique to question.

It was Lacy's turn to be somewhat embarrassed. No matter what the circumstances, she still owed Megan a great deal. "Yes, but still—''

"Thanks aren't necessary,'' Megan repeated, her eyes kind as they washed over Lacy. "For any of it. So—'' she handed Connor a cup and then gave one to Lacy before picking up her own "—any plans yet?''

Taking a sip, Megan kept her eyes on the younger woman. She'd all but made up her mind about Lacy, deciding that she was one of the good ones. A little defensive perhaps, but who could blame her? The girl had had more than her share of bad breaks. But all that was going to change.

Lacy shook her head. So much had happened, she was having trouble assimilating it all. "Catching my breath first.''

Megan smiled, her eyes shifting to her son. Connor didn't look too happy. His brooding expression reminded her so much of Clyde, the ranch hand who had captured her heart at seventeen, only to desert her when she needed him most. But for all that, there was no denying that he had been exquisite to look at.

"Always a wise thing to do," she said to Lacy.

Lacy took Chase's bib off and set it on the table. The high chair's small tray was far too messy. "And then I guess I'll be taking him home with me."

Megan's heart felt as if it had stopped midbeat, though she tried to give no indication. "And home would be...?"

Lacy picked up a sponge and cleaned off the tray, lifting Chase's splayed hands one at a time to finish the job. Cereal and the fruit she'd added to the mix were on his fingers, evidence of his enthusiastic attempts at feeding himself. She thought Megan knew where she lived. "Why, the room I have now at the boarding house."

Megan released the breath she'd been holding. It had already been established that Lacy was Chase's mother. She'd taken the simple lab test eagerly. Fighting for custody of the baby wasn't in her, but Megan's heart would have broken if she drastically lost Chase out of her everyday life. "Thank God, I was afraid you meant someplace else." She saw that Lacy didn't follow her. "Where you came from originally."

Lacy shook her head, deliberately not looking in

Connor's direction. The ranch was gone. "I've no reason to go back."

Even if Connor planned on returning to the area, she added silently. Whatever had brought him to Austin and the Maitlands was probably only temporary, and when it was over, he'd go back. And she would remain here, making a life for herself and her son.

She tried to ignore the sharp prick she felt in her heart.

Megan could feel the tension in the room. There was so much she wanted to say to Lacy. To both of them. But that would be getting ahead of herself. It was all set for this evening. No matter how upside down everything until now had been, this one revelation had to proceed according to the order she'd decided on.

Still, she felt impatience goading her. Trying to distract herself, she looked at Lacy, then nodded at Chase. "May I?"

If I could give my son a grandmother, Lacy thought, *the woman would be one exactly like Megan Maitland.* "Of course."

Megan slowly lifted Chase from his high chair. He greeted her efforts with a wide grin. A sweetness pressed against her chest as she held him to her.

Her grandson.

She still could hardly believe it was true.

Turning to Lacy, she placed a hand on the young

woman's arm. "All I ask is that you make no decisions about anything until tonight."

That sounded very mysterious. Without meaning to, Lacy glanced in Connor's direction. There was nothing in his expression to enlighten her. "Tonight?"

Megan patted Chase on the back, rubbing in small concentric circles. With so much on her mind, Lacy had obviously forgotten, she thought. "I'm having the family over for an informal dinner. To celebrate Chase's recovery." She saw the light dawn on Lacy's face. "And I have a few things to announce." Only one of which was important to her, she added silently. But she didn't want to give away any more than was necessary. "Also, I want to hear all the details that were glossed over last night." She looked at Connor. "Everything," she emphasized.

What was she driving at? he wondered. She already knew everything that seemed pertinent. Petey was dead and Janelle was behind bars. What more was there?

"Such as?" His tone was naturally wary.

"Such as there are pieces missing from this puzzle. Important pieces." Megan saw by the look on his face that he wanted her to be more specific. But she didn't want to launch into that now. She wanted to wait until they were all together. "But I'll contain my curiosity until tonight." She turned to Lacy. Though none of what Lacy had gone through this past year was her fault, she wanted to make things up to the girl. "Right now, I think we need to get this big boy changed and ready to go."

"Go? Go where?" Lacy asked.

"Shopping," Megan replied brightly. She held Chase in the air, and the baby gurgled, shoving his fist into his mouth. The drool that followed told Megan another tooth was coming in soon. "I think in honor of his being officially recognized as a Maitland, he needs to get additions to his wardrobe befitting his station in life." Laughing, she inclined her head toward Lacy. "Humor me, I feel like lavishing money and attention on him—and his mother."

Lacy wasn't about to accept charity, not even from someone as nice as Megan. "Oh, no, that's not necessary. You've already bought so much for Chase, I—"

Megan wasn't about to put up with excuses. "The only thing that's necessary," Megan told her, cutting Lacy off, "is for you to pack away your pride and say yes. Pride's all well and good in its place, but it's a poor substitute for having things. Take it from a woman who knows." She saw the skeptical look on Lacy's face. "There was a time that church mice thought of me as being poorer than they were."

Lacy couldn't believe that Megan had experienced anything less than living in the lap of luxury. "You?"

"Me." A tinge of pride entered Megan's voice.

"When I married William Maitland, his family thought he'd taken leave of his senses and that I would drag him down." Her smile was sunny, almost transforming her into the young woman who had caught William's eye and heart. "I turned out to be the best thing that ever happened to him and his stodgy family." Megan winked at both of them. "Or so he liked to tell me. Now come along, no more excuses or dragging your feet."

"Yes, ma'am."

"There, that's what I like to hear. Complete compliance." She glanced over her shoulder at Connor just before she and Lacy left the room with Chase. "You could stand to learn a thing or two from this girl, Connor."

He already had, he thought, watching them leave. And that was just the problem.

CHAPTER THREE

"WELL, WELL, WELL, aren't you the little princess?"

Straightening her shoulders, Janelle tossed her hair over her shoulder, its deep chestnut color a sharp contrast to the drab prison-gray dress she was wearing.

Her lips curled in an expression that was half smirk, half sneer as she regarded the visitor the guard had ushered her in to see. If she'd been expecting Connor, she gave no indication of her disappointment. Instead, brassy insolence defined every inch of her countenance.

She dropped into the chair that faced Lacy's across the visitor's table, determined to remain in control over the other woman the way she had all along. "I was wondering if you'd get around to coming to see me."

Alone in the small five-by-nine room with Janelle, Lacy knew there was a policeman right outside the door. All she had to do was call and the man would instantly be in the room, ready to stop anything that was happening. Janelle couldn't hurt her anymore.

Couldn't steal her baby away the way she had twice already.

But logic didn't really help quell the uneasiness shimmering through her.

With effort, Lacy drew her courage to her. Cutting the shopping trip short, she had left Chase in Megan's care with a fabricated excuse, borrowed a car from her and driven to the police precinct where she knew Janelle was being kept until her arraignment. She was determined to get some answers from the woman. Otherwise, the questions would continue to haunt her, creeping in late at night, wrapped up in nightmares.

"Why?" The single word echoed between them. Janelle looked disinterested. Lacy raised her voice. "Why did you do all this?"

Janelle laughed shortly, pretending to regard her nails. The polish had chipped off them, leaving dull spots here and there. "If you can't figure that out, you're simpler than I thought."

Janelle's contemptuous tone ate at her, but then, she hadn't come here expecting civility.

"For the money, I know that. I know all about your husband posing as Connor. I can even understand, when it looked as if it was all going to go up in flames, why you stole Chase." Lacy leaned across the table, her eyes intent on Janelle. "But why did you try to steal him from me in the first place? I was no threat to you."

Janelle's lips twisted, deepening the sneer. She ached to rake what was left of her nails across the pale, delicate face, scarring it. "A lot you know. You were a threat from the very first second you decided to make a play for Connor."

Lacy stood her ground. "I didn't make a play, that just happened."

"Yeah, right." Cynicism dripped from every syllable. Innocence and love in their purest sense had never existed in Janelle's world. They were myths, fairy tales she'd never witnessed firsthand. "I figured the kid would make a good prop—and I was right. The second she saw him, the old lady melted all over the little bastard—and I use the word correctly," she added with a malicious laugh, seeing Lacy's inadvertent wince.

An icy hand passed over her heart. Lacy shivered. She'd never realized how truly evil Janelle was until this moment. "And you were willing to kill me to get him?"

The shrug was careless, dismissive. Lacy was less than dirt to her. "Hey, a girl's gotta do what a girl's gotta do. You'd given birth to the brat, you'd served your purpose." Janelle's eyes narrowed as she looked at the younger woman. "That made you expendable."

Anger flooded Lacy. This woman had held her baby captive. Who was to say what she would have done to him if she'd suddenly thought of him as expendable? "And what gives you the right to play with people's lives like that?"

"The right?" Janelle echoed. A savage hatred came into her eyes. "The right?" She reached across the table and grabbed Lacy's arm, her fingers digging into her flesh. "I'll tell you what gives me the right. I'm one of them, damn it." Incensed, she released her hold as if she were tossing Lacy away from her. "And while they go around getting everything they want, money dripping out of their pockets, I'm supposed to do without? The hell I am."

Lacy stared at her. "One of them? What are you talking about? How can you be one of them?"

Her anger under control, Janelle laughed coldly. She liked having all the answers. Doling them out. It made her feel powerful.

"Surprises you, does it? Well, Connor's squeaky-clean family has a few skeletons in their closet. My father was the old lady's brother-in-law. Robert Maitland." There was no love in her voice as she said her father's name, just as there had never been any love in her heart for the man who'd given her life, but little else.

Lacy thought she had her there. "Robert Maitland had two children he abandoned, R.J. and Anna."

Megan had filled her in on the family history during lunch today. Taking Chase with them, they'd dined in one of Austin's better restaurants, and Megan had made a point of clearing things up for her.

Until then, Lacy had thought that R.J. and Anna were Megan's oldest children. She'd been surprised to discover that they, like Connor, were nephew and niece. Megan and her late husband had adopted the two after their widowed father, Robert, had disappeared one day. The magnitude of Megan's heart had impressed Lacy.

Just as the meanness within Janelle's took her breath away.

Janelle's lips narrowed into two thin lines. "Surprise—he married my mother and then abandoned four more kids before he finally cashed in his chips. You'll pardon the expression," she said sarcastically when she saw the confusion on Lacy's face. "I'm from Vegas. That's where Robert Maitland met my mother." For just a fraction of a second, she looked away and her expression softened. If she had ever felt anything at all, it had been for her mother. "My mother was a showgirl. She was really something in her prime." And then her face clouded over, malevolent again. "But he had no use for her after her looks started to go."

Janelle's gaze shifted back to Lacy. "That's a Maitland for you—takes the best, leaves the rest." Anger flashed in her eyes. She wanted revenge on all of them. "They owe me. And when I found that letter from Big Daddy Harland to 'Uncle' William in my father's things after he died, I figured it was time the Maitlands paid up."

Lacy wasn't following this. What Janelle was saying was so disjointed, part of her thought the other woman was deranged or making things up. "What letter?"

Because it had been such an integral part of her scam for the past year, Janelle had momentarily forgotten it was still a secret.

"You don't know, do you? You don't know who you've been drooling over. He's—" And then she realized that she had another weapon in her hand. Something to hold over Lacy's head. Her eyes glinted as her thoughts scrambled. "No, never mind. Why should you know? Why should I tell you anything? Unless, of course," she continued loftily, "you can see your way clear to using your influence with that old bitch and getting the charges against me dropped."

It was a trick, a ploy. There was no so-called secret, no letter. It was just Janelle's way of trying to manipulate her again. But she wasn't the same person she'd been a year ago, Lacy thought. She was her own person now.

It was Lacy's turn to be contemptuous. And to look at Janelle with pity. "I don't have any influence, and even if I did, I wouldn't use it. Not to get you off. You're evil, Janelle."

If the words were meant to shame Janelle, they fell far short of their mark. Instead, she laughed, amused. "Damn straight I am—and proud of it.

What did being a Goody Two-shoes ever get anyone?''

Lacy rose to her feet and crossed to the door.
There was no anger, no hatred any longer. There was
only abject pity in her eyes as she looked at Janelle.
Instead of trying to make something of herself, she'd
destroyed lives and created a wretched future for herself, all because she'd been consumed with envy.

''Peace of mind,'' Lacy answered quietly. She
rapped on the door, then stepped back as it was
opened. ''I'm ready to go now.''

''Go ahead, go,'' Janelle scoffed, waving her
away. ''But you'll be back. You'll come crawling
back, begging me to tell you. Wait and see if you
don't,'' Janelle called after her before the door
closed, sealing her in a world she'd never foreseen
for herself.

As SHE DROVE away from the jail, her mind in turmoil, Lacy's first thought was to go to Connor with
what she'd just discovered.

But he'd been so distant since last night. Would
he think she was making it all up for some purpose
of her own? Not that she could entirely blame him.
After being exposed to the likes of Janelle, Connor
probably held everything suspect. He might not believe what she had to tell him, especially since she
hadn't told him about his son.

But that was exactly why he should believe her,

she argued silently. The very fact that she hadn't told him he had a son should prove that she wasn't out for anything, certainly not her own personal gain.

She needed proof before she went to Connor.

Lacy realized that the light had turned green and there were cars behind her, waiting to go. The one directly behind her beeped. She pressed down on the gas pedal.

What had Janelle meant when she'd implied that Connor wasn't who he seemed to be? Was there a germ of truth in that, or was Janelle just trying to mess up her mind?

Probably the latter.

But she couldn't quite put her mind to rest on the subject.

Lacy blew out a breath. Glancing at the street sign on the corner, she made a decision. At the end of the block, she made a U-turn. Before she let her imagination get the better of her and gave Janelle's rantings any credence, she wanted to have a few things cleared up. But for that, she was going to need some help.

And she knew just who to go to.

"YOU'RE ASKING ME to give away my secrets?" Chelsea asked, half in jest.

"Not all of them," Lacy clarified, not sure if she'd offended Chelsea. She hardly knew the woman, and this probably seemed like an imposition. "I just need to know where to find some information. I need to have something substantiated.'' Chelsea had, until recently, worked for the tabloid television show ''Tattle Today TV.'' Lacy was certain that if anyone would know where to find old records, it would be Chelsea.

Chelsea slipped her arm around the other woman's shoulders, drawing her into the cozy living room of Max Jamison's house. The TV reporter and private investigator had finally acknowledged their love for each other after a year of being each other's worst enemies.

''I'm teasing, Lacy,'' Chelsea said. ''You have to lighten up a little, although Lord knows you've had more than your share to deal with lately. Sure, I'll help. Just what is it you need to know?''

She led Lacy to a room just down the hall. Inside Lacy could see a desk with a laptop computer on it. The screen was turned on. ''Is there somewhere on the Internet I can look up marriage licenses and birth records?''

And here she'd thought Lacy was going to ask something difficult. Chelsea almost felt cheated of a challenge. ''Provided they're available, sure.'' She led her into the room Max used as an office. ''Got a name?''

''Yes,'' Lucy said, entering behind her.

''State?'' Standing to the side of the desk, Chelsea turned to look at Lacy. ''Or better yet, a city?''

"Yes." But what if Janelle had been lying about where she was from? "At least, I think so."

"Great, then you're in business." Leaning over the computer, Chelsea pressed a few buttons, hooking up to the Internet. A tinny voice announced that she had mail. Chelsea grinned. "You know, in a few years, we're probably going to be able to walk up to this little box and say, 'Computer, access birth records from—'" She looked at Lacy.

"Las Vegas."

Curiosity began to unfurl within her, but Chelsea held it in check. "Las Vegas and, wham, it'll all be there, right at your fingertips." She gestured at the screen. "Who would have ever thought that Gene Rodenberry was a visionary?"

Lacy looked at her blankly. "Who?"

Chelsea's expression was incredulous. "My God, girl, don't tell me you've never seen an episode of *Star Trek*? That's almost un-American."

Concerned with the import of what she might have learned, Lacy knew her mind was a million miles away. She flushed. "Oh, right. The producer. Sorry, I guess I'm a little preoccupied at the moment."

With what? Chelsea wondered. "No problem, I understand." She cleared away a few papers, then stepped back, letting Lacy sit down at the desk. "Now, want me to hover around as a consultant, or do you want to do this in private?"

Lacy bit her lower lip, hesitating. This was Chelsea's laptop. She couldn't very well tell her to go away. On the other hand, she didn't want to have to be in a position to deal with questions before she was sure she had the right answers. "I—"

Chelsea had gone far in her field because of her acute ability to read a person's body language and subtle shifts in mood. She saw her answer in Lacy's eyes.

"Gotcha." She smiled. "I'm into privacy a lot more since I've left 'Tattle Today.'" Moving in closer for a second, she typed something on the upper portion of the screen, then stepped aside again. "Okay, there's the Web address. Have fun."

Chelsea left and closed the door behind her, consumed with curiosity but bound by her word. Sometimes, she mused, being honorable had its drawbacks.

MEGAN COULDN'T help herself. Having finished dressing for dinner, she stopped by Lacy's room and rapped lightly before peeking in.

What she saw warmed her heart. The inner loveliness she'd been aware of since the first moment she'd met Lacy was most definitely shining through.

"You certainly are a knockout." Circling the other woman slowly, Megan nodded. "I knew that dress was perfect for you the second we saw it in the store window."

Pleased, Lacy ran her hands over the skirt of the sheath she was wearing. The amount on the price tag she'd glimpsed while trying it on in the store was more than her entire wardrobe had cost back when she'd worked as a cook for Connor and his mother on their ranch.

But Megan had insisted on buying it for her, and Lacy couldn't seem to make herself resist. She had already turned down Megan's generosity several times. It was one thing for the woman to buy clothes for her grandnephew, but Lacy knew she wasn't anything to the family. Just a woman caught up in things, nothing more.

Still, the gesture touched her heart, just as the dress had won it.

Beaming, Lacy turned to catch a glimpse of herself in the mirror. The deep green sheath was beautiful. "I'll pay you back as soon as I can."

"Don't you dare," Megan warned sternly. "I'll be extremely hurt if you do, Lacy. One of the nice things about having money is that I get to spend it the way I want on the people I want. Now stop being difficult and smile, dear. You look positively radiant when you do." When the shy smile appeared, Megan nodded, pleased. "Easy to see why Connor lost his head over you."

The misbegotten observation sobered her. "Connor didn't lose his head," Lacy corrected Megan quietly. "He was grief-stricken over the loss of his mother and he'd had a little too much to drink that night."

As she spoke, it all came vividly back to her. The words, the moment, the look in his eyes as he took her into his arms and kissed her. She could almost feel his lips on hers. She'd never felt so happy in her life. Before or since.

"When I tried to comfort him, well, one thing just seemed to lead to another...." She let her voice drift off.

Megan tried to read between the lines and wasn't sure she liked what she was reading. "He forced himself on you?"

Lacy's mouth dropped open. "Oh, no, no," she protested quickly. "He's never been anything but a complete gentleman." A sad smile teased the corners of her mouth. "A little too much so. I've always had feelings for him, but it was sort of a one-way street."

Relieved that her grandchild hadn't been conceived as a result of an assault, Megan smiled at the young woman beside her.

"I'm not so sure." She'd seen the way Connor had looked at Lacy in unguarded moments. Seen the way he'd behaved toward her when Lacy had rushed out last night to claim her son. There was far more than just chivalry at work here.

Not wanting her hopes to rise needlessly, Lacy waved away Megan's words. "You're just being kind."

No, she wasn't, but she didn't have time to make

Lacy see reason. Her children had been arriving for the last half hour. It was time to get things moving.

"We'll discuss this later," Megan promised. "Right now, I want to get that son of yours and bring him downstairs to dinner."

"He's a little young to handle a wineglass," Lacy quipped.

"We'll improvise," Megan promised, leading the way.

MEGAN HAD hardly touched her dinner, but sat watching the others eat theirs. Wondering if she was making a mistake by calling her children together tonight. But she had no choice. Too much time had lapsed already, time she would never get back. She'd have to make up for it by using the present and the future.

At her elbow, her son Mitchell inclined his head, catching her attention. "You seem nervous tonight, Mother," he noted. "Is anything wrong?"

"Yes, why the formal gathering?" R.J. asked. She'd been very mysterious in her invitation, letting none of them know what was going on.

"It's an informal gathering," Megan corrected. Setting down her fork, she gave up the pretense that she was eating. Less than two morsels had passed her lips.

"If you say so," R.J. replied, taking a sip from his water glass. "So why are we here informally?"

"Yes, Mother." Anna couldn't stand the secrecy any longer. "What's going on?"

There were butterflies in her stomach, Megan realized. That hadn't happened to her in a very long time. She'd grown accustomed to dealing with life head-on instead of wasting time with such trivial things as nerves. But this involved her family. Her children.

Her eyes swept slowly over all seven of their faces. R.J., Anna, Mitch, Abby, Jake, Beth and Ellie. The butterflies took another pass. Other than Ellie and Connor, her children thought this was about celebrating Chase's return. They hadn't a clue as to why she'd called them here and what she was going to say.

Would she wind up turning their worlds upside down? Would they bring themselves to forgive her youthful indiscretion?

She could only hope so.

Spreading her hands on the table, Megan took a deep breath. "I've gathered you all together because I wanted to make an announcement and I wanted you all to find out at the same time." Pausing, she was tempted to look at Ellie, but she resisted.

"You've found a man and you're getting married," Jake teased.

"Jake!" Ellie cried. Everyone knew how faithful their mother was to the memory of their father. That she could even look at anyone else was unthinkable.

"Well, why not?" he asked. "We all seem to have been pairing off pretty regularly this last year. Maybe there's something in the water." The corners of his mouth lifted in a teasing smile. "Maybe Mom drank it, too." He turned to look at her. "So, how about it, Mom? Is there someone new on the horizon we should be getting ready to call Dad?"

"My money's on Hugh," Mitchell said. Hugh Blake had been the family's lawyer for more years than any of them could remember. "I've seen the way he looks at you, Mother. Definitely smitten."

"No, this isn't about Hugh." But there *was* someone new on the horizon. Someone they should be getting ready to call brother, she thought silently. Fingers icy, she began. "You all know that your father and I started Maitland Maternity so that young women who found themselves pregnant and alone would have somewhere to go. Somewhere along the line, the clinic became a trendy, *in* place to have a baby, and I'm not quite sure why that is, but the fact that it happened is beside the point." She saw the question in their eyes. They were wondering where she was going with this. "What you don't know is why the hospital was founded."

Confused, Abby looked at Beth, who shrugged. "You just told us, Mother—"

"Not the whole reason." She realized that she'd been folding and refolding her napkin and forced herself to stop. "It was started because I didn't want anyone to have to go through what I had gone through.''

R.J. glanced at Mitchell, then at his mother. ''But you were married.''

Megan moistened her lips. ''Not when I was pregnant with my first child.''

Abby grinned. So that was it. Their mother was going to confess being human to them. It seemed sweetly old-fashioned. ''You mean you and Dad danced the light fantastic before he married you?''

It was now or never. ''I was seventeen years old and very much in love.''

''But you're sixty-two,'' Beth protested. ''If you were seventeen when you were pregnant for the first time, that would make Mitchell, what? Forty-five?''

There was an apology in her eyes as Megan looked at Mitchell. ''Mitchell is not my firstborn.'' Her glance shifted briefly to Connor before she dropped her bombshell. ''Connor is.''

CHAPTER FOUR

IT WAS QUIET enough to hear the proverbial pin drop. Certainly quiet enough to hear the spoon that slipped from Lacy's suddenly lax fingers, landing on her plate with a clatter.

So that was what Janelle had been hinting at, Lacy realized. Janelle knew. Somehow, the other woman had discovered that Connor wasn't Clarise's son but Megan's.

That had to be what the letter was about, the one she'd started to say she'd found among her father's things. Why hadn't she pressed Janelle further when she'd had the chance?

Reflexively covering the spoon with her hand, Lacy met Megan's eyes and offered the woman who had befriended her so easily an apologetic half-smile. She could have sworn she saw a touch of gratitude in the other woman's eyes just before they left hers and swept over the other occupants of the tomb-silent dining room.

You could almost hear the light emerging from the chandelier overhead, Megan thought. There were varying degrees of shock and astonishment registered on her children's faces. What she didn't see, she realized, was condemnation or any looks of dismay.

It was too early to entertain relief, but she made a mental reservation.

It was Mitchell who found his tongue first. Slanting a glance at Connor, he then addressed his mother. "How…how is that possible, Mother?"

Though she'd thought him dead, she'd never stopped loving her first child. And never stopped feeling the weight of the secret she'd silently carried around with her all these years.

She folded her hands before her primly, fortifying herself with the small, formal action. It kept her hands from trembling.

"It's possible, Mitchell, because it's true." And then, very slowly, she began to bare her soul to the people who mattered most in her life. They had a right to know. It was past time. "Forty-six years ago, when I was just seventeen and very naive, I believed a tall, strapping, good-looking ranch hand when he said he loved me. That he couldn't live without me." Her lips curved sadly at the thought of the trusting, vulnerable young girl she'd once been. "As it turned out, he could. Easily. He proved it the moment he discovered I was pregnant." She eased herself past the shell of pain that still lingered, even after all this time. "In one of those funny little twists of life, he turned out to be a very distant cousin of the Maitlands', disgruntled and bitter at the way life had left him in the shadows while shining down on Harland Maitland and his family.

"But none of that mattered to me. What did was that I was pregnant and determined to have my baby even though my father tried to convince me to find a way to 'shed my problem.'" It was her father's euphemism, not hers. There was a fresh emptiness in her heart. Her father had sold her baby. Megan didn't know if she was ever going to be able to forgive him. "When I wouldn't follow his advice, he decided to take matters into his own hands. The day I gave birth quickly became the saddest day of my life." Unconsciously, she raised her chin, still needing to stave off the pain the memory generated. "My father told me my baby had been born dead." Megan felt tears gathering, and she struggled to keep them back. "I was sure it was somehow my fault. I had no way of knowing that my father had sold his own grandson to Harland Maitland, who turned around and presented that baby to his only daughter, Clarise, and her husband, Jack O'Hara."

She wanted to look at Connor, to see his expression as she made these revelations to everyone. To see if she could glean how he felt.

But she was afraid to. Afraid he was still bonded to Clarise and would resent her for any perceived criticism of the only mother he'd ever known. Or that the entire experience of being lied to had left him hollow and lacking any emotions at all.

Jake ran his hand along the back of his neck. The hairs there were prickling. "So how did you discover what happened?"

After having the family beset by a legion of women, all claiming that Chase was the product of a union between them and one of the Maitland men, including him, he held any revelation suspect at the moment. He'd taken a liking to Connor, had been there when the original deception about the false Connor had been uncovered. But this was asking all of them to take a giant leap of faith.

"There's a paper trail," Megan answered, and she thanked God for it. Otherwise, who knew how long they would all be in limbo while this was being untangled and verified? "The secret apparently was too much for Harland to bear, and just before his death he put everything down in two letters, one for William and one for Clarise. Somehow Jack intercepted the letter for Clarise and found out the baby was mine. That's when he engineered a rift with William and took Clarise and their son, *my* son—" she had to add that, needed to make the distinction "—and moved away. By this time Connor was already three, and Jack must have figured Clarise would be devastated to give the baby up. Apparently Clarise didn't find out the truth until her husband died when Connor was sixteen. Even then she chose not to tell her son the whole story, but wrote him a letter and entrusted it, with Harland's letter, to her lawyer, instructing both to be delivered on the first anniversary of her death.''

Megan sighed and looked regretfully at Connor. "I should never have believed Petey when he claimed to be you, but his version of what happened was exactly the same as yours, and you have Clarise's letter to prove it.''

Megan had tried putting herself in Clarise's place, all those years ago, and she could understand the woman's actions. Clarise was probably afraid that Connor might curse her memory and Jack's once he discovered the deception about his birth.

While he sympathized with what his mother had to be going through, making this painful revelation to them, R.J. still harbored a few doubts about the situation. "If you don't mind my asking, how can we be sure that this Connor is *the* Connor and not just another impostor?''

In true motherly fashion, Megan came to his defense. "Connor has already submitted to a test to prove his paternity, something, if you recall, Janelle kept postponing.'' Looking back, Megan felt embarrassed at how easily she'd been duped by the duo. But that had been because she'd been so stunned by the news and so eager to take her son to her heart. Looking at Connor, she *knew* he was her son. "As soon as Lacy regained her memory and told Connor that the baby was his, we asked him to submit to a buccal test, and he was more than happy to do it.

None of us could afford to have any more paternity mix-ups.''

''How did Janelle and her husband know about Connor being alive when you didn't?'' Abby wanted to know.

Megan shook her head. ''Somehow they got hold of Harland's letter to William, but how, I don't know—though I definitely intend to find out.''

''I think I have an idea.''

Everyone, including Connor, turned to look at Lacy when she spoke.

''You do?'' Megan queried. ''What do you mean, Lacy?''

''I went to see Janelle today. When I left Chase with you,'' she explained.

She'd asked Megan if she could leave the baby at the clinic's day-care center for a few hours. Megan had quickly volunteered to take the rest of the afternoon off and play grandmother, giving Lacy the use of her car. In the generosity of spirit that defined her, Megan had asked no questions. At the time, Lacy had felt as if she was deceiving her by being deliberately vague. But she'd been afraid that if she told Megan her plans, Megan would forbid her from going to see Janelle.

Lacy made her confession. ''That was the errand I had to run.''

It was Connor, not Megan, who expressed disapproval. ''You went to the jail?''

Lacy tried not to let his tone affect her. Much as she loved him, Connor had no say in her life. He'd given up any rights to orchestrate her life when he'd distanced himself from her.

Lacy raised her chin defensively. "There were things I had to find out."

Megan sensed this was escalating into a confrontation and intervened. "What did you find out about the second letter—the one that must have been for William?" she asked Lacy.

Relieved to get back to the subject, Lacy said, "Janelle told me she found it amid her father's things after he died."

Confused, R.J. looked at the others. The story was beginning to take on epic proportions. "Who's her father? Or was?" he amended.

Lacy took a deep breath. This was going to come as a shock to him and his sister more than to the others. "Robert Maitland. Janelle's your half sister."

Anna and R.J. blanched as they looked at each other.

"What is this, another one of Janelle's tricks?" Connor demanded.

This was going too far, he thought. Somehow, Janelle had stumbled across a genealogy of his family and was fabricating things right and left to serve her own ends. He'd had his fill of the lies that had infiltrated his life ever since Janelle had entered it. She'd been his mother's companion at the end, and he'd initially been grateful to her for making Clarise's life more tolerable. But her subsequent actions negated that.

"No," Lacy countered firmly. She could see by his expression that she'd surprised Connor. "It's true. I looked up the birth and marriage certificates in the Las Vegas records—that's where Janelle was born," she added. She felt like she was stumbling over her own tongue, the words tumbling out haphazardly. This wasn't the way she'd wanted to tell them, but facing this formidable family made it difficult to think clearly, even if they were friendly for the most part. "I asked Chelsea to help me."

"Chelsea knows?" Anna's heart sank. Chelsea had only recently walked away from her television job. Would the prospect of unearthing yet another scandal surrounding the Maitlands prove to be too much of a temptation to resist?

"Only that I was trying to find birth certificates," Lacy replied quickly. "I didn't tell her why or whose. And she didn't ask," she added in the woman's defense. Lacy looked at Megan, hoping she would understand. "I wanted to tell you first, but I didn't want to come to you until I was sure that Janelle wasn't making all of this up for some reason."

Jake, looking decidedly uncomfortable, turned to his mother. "Lacy's right, Mom. We found out the same info when we ran a check on Janelle's fingerprints. I should have warned you, but so much was happening, there never seemed to be a right time. We decided to wait until we had confirmed Chase's paternity—and then he was kidnapped.''

Megan could hardly speak. The thought that someone in the Maitland family was capable of these kinds of sinister machinations was difficult for her to reconcile. Hurt and saddened, she could only shake her head. She knew that a desire for money was at the bottom of all this. If Janelle had just come to her honestly, things could have been so different.

''Where is Robert?'' she asked Lacy.

''He's dead.'' Lacy hated being the one who had to tell her. ''He and his wife were killed in Las Vegas some time ago.''

''Car accident?'' Mitch guessed. He looked at Anna and R.J., wondering how deeply this affected them.

''No.'' Lacy shook her head. She'd gone through the death certificates, as well, just in case Janelle had lied about her father being dead. ''They were gunned down in back of a casino, probably for a gambling debt.''

Stunned, Megan looked at Anna and R.J. She'd thought of them as her own children for so long, it was difficult to remember that they really weren't. ''I'm sorry, my darlings.''

R.J. shook his head, touched by what he saw in his mother's eyes. ''Don't be. He stopped being our father a long time ago, even before he left us. William was our father.''

Anna nodded her agreement. ''And we couldn't have had a better one.''

Megan smiled her thanks. ''I'll have Max look into this further,'' she promised. ''That should help satisfy Chelsea's curiosity, which I know must be bursting. Not that I don't believe you,'' she added quickly, looking at Lacy and Jake. ''I just want to make sure this somehow isn't just another clever twist on that girl's part.'' She sighed, remembering. ''There've been so many lies this last year, it's hard to keep sight of what's true and what isn't.''

''Speaking of which,'' Abby interjected, ''do we send out birth announcements, or what?'' When her mother looked at her quizzically, Abby indicated Connor with raised eyebrows.

Relief flooded through Megan, warm and cleansing. She knew by Abby's question that at least Abby had welcomed Connor as her brother.

One look at the faces gathered around her told Megan that they had all accepted Connor. Why had she ever doubted them?

She unfolded the hands she had been squeezing together so tightly and smiled. ''I don't know, that depends on you.''

Mitchell pretended to give his new sibling the once-over, then laughed. ''He's a little big for that, don't you think?''

"You never get too big to be told that you're an important member of this family," Jake interjected, raising a glass in Connor's direction.

Ellie, seated closest to Connor, leaned over and placed her hand on his forearm. "I am so glad that the secret is finally out and I can stop worrying about letting it slip accidentally."

"You knew?" Beth asked, stunned.

"I wasn't supposed to. I overheard," Ellie admitted to her twin before looking at Connor again. "I guess it's goodbye cousin, hello brother." She grinned broadly at his slightly bemused expression. "Welcome to the family, Connor."

He wasn't certain how he was supposed to react to that. Or to any of them. This was all very new to him.

Suddenly, they were on their feet, surrounding him, pulling him up and shaking his hand, or in Abby's case, embracing him. Their voices blended into one another until all Connor was aware of was a din buzzing about his ears.

And his mother smiling at all of them.

At him.

It felt so strange to him. He'd lost one mother, a mother he cared about a great deal, almost two years ago, only to discover that she had lied to him. She hadn't been his mother at all, and he had another mother, his real mother, who was still alive.

Would he be able to trust anyone again? Connor

had no answer for that. He knew what his heart said, but his heart was still too raw to listen to.

And then Megan was beside him, her arm threaded through his, a wide, almost beatific smile on her lips. Maybe, in time, it would work itself all out, he thought. Until then, he'd just let things ride and be an observer.

Megan's eyes were smarting as she watched her other children open their arms and their hearts to this man who was in fact a stranger to them, all embracing him because he was part of her. Her heart swelled within her mother's breast. They were a good bunch, these children of hers.

Abby leaned in to her until her cheek was touching Megan's. "Are you crying, Mother?"

Overhearing, Jake didn't wait for her answer. He dug into his pocket and slipped his mother a handkerchief.

Nodding her gratitude, Megan dabbed at her eyes. "We did a good job, your father and I, raising all of you." She folded the handkerchief and handed it back to Jake. "You've done me proud tonight."

"Nothing less than you deserve, Mom," Beth assured her quietly.

Jake slipped his arm around his mother's waist, pulling her closer. When she looked at him in surprise, he asked in a stage whisper, "So, Mom, is there anything else we should know?"

"A secret life as an international jewel thief, perhaps?" Abby asked, suppressing a grin.

"No secret life," Megan swore, crossing her heart. "And no other secrets—among any of us."

"Well, I for one am relieved everything's out in the open," Jake declared, pressing a kiss to her temple.

Standing on the sidelines, Lacy watched Connor's reaction to this emotional outpouring. Anyone else might have looked overjoyed, but not Connor. If anything, he seemed uncomfortable at the attention his newfound family was giving him. If he had his druthers, she knew he would have preferred to vanish.

That made them different, she thought. If she had just discovered that she had a big, loving family willing to welcome her with open arms, she would have felt like singing. He looked as if he felt like fleeing.

But then, Connor had always been a loner. Clarise had seen to that. He'd been so loyal to her, he hadn't realized that she'd given him a twisted sense of what was important in life. Lacy had a feeling that Clarise had never taught Connor to take pleasure in the simple joy that being around people who loved you brought.

Looking at the people around him now, she could only think that Connor didn't realize how lucky he was.

Their eyes met across the table.

Having caught her attention, he nodded toward the side, indicating that he wanted to talk to her.

Probably to upbraid her for going to talk to Janelle after everything that had happened, Lacy thought. She knew he considered the other woman dangerous and obviously felt Lacy couldn't handle herself.

Not that he had proof to the contrary, Lacy mused. After all, Janelle had manipulated her. But Janelle had managed to manipulate everyone to a greater or lesser degree. And besides, that was the old Lacy. She'd done a lot of growing this past year. Never mind that some of it had been as Sara, the woman she'd been when her memory was gone. She'd kept with her all the experiences that Sara had gone through, all the lessons that Sara had learned. They had helped forge a backbone for her that wasn't easily bent.

Not even for a man she loved.

Politely extracting himself from these strangers who had become, through the whimsy of fate, his siblings, Connor sidestepped his mother. Megan took his place in the center of the circle, filling the void. He expected nothing less. Ever since he'd arrived here, it seemed to Connor that there had been endless talking and activity around him.

The Maitlands certainly didn't value their quiet time, he thought.

Taking Lacy by the arm, he guided her out of the

room to the adjacent living room, mercifully leaving the din behind.

"I need to talk to you."

He sounded tense. Despite promises to herself to let him have his say and remain calm, Lacy felt her back go up.

"If this is about going to see Janelle—"

He cut her off before she could start. "No, this isn't about going to see Janelle." He set his jaw. "It's about the future. Yours and mine."

Connor's stoic expression baffled her. Lacy hadn't a clue what he was trying to say. "You know, for a man who's just been taken into the bosom of a loving family, you don't look like you feel very happy."

He was honest with her. Of everyone in the house, she was the one who at least had a history with him. As well as a son.

Knowing he had a child only added to his tangled web of emotions.

"I don't know what I feel right now. Confused, mostly," he admitted before his face hardened again. "But that's my problem."

He was shutting her out again. Why did she expect anything different? Lacy silently upbraided herself. "Right, I remember. You're very big about defining borders. I won't trespass on your problem." For two cents, she would have taken her fists and beaten some sense into his hard head. "Now what is it you want to talk to me about?"

He thought of the deed that was still hot in his pocket. "I bought a ranch this afternoon."

Lacy could only stare at him. He hadn't said anything to anyone about wanting to buy property. "You did what?"

"Bought a ranch," he repeated. "It's down the road from Garrett Lord's place." Garrett had gone with him to look at it. It had taken only ten minutes for him to make up his mind. They'd gone to a lawyer to draw up papers this afternoon. "The guy who owned it had been thinking about selling it for a long time, and I figured that since I've just found my real mother, maybe I should stick around here for the time being. There's nothing for me in Montana."

"Montana? Is that where you went off to?" He'd disappeared right after she'd left the ranch. No wonder it had been impossible for her to contact him once she'd decided to give it one last try.

Montana. Somehow, that suited him, she thought. Vast stretches of land where you wouldn't come across another living soul if you didn't want to. It was Connor's kind of country.

"Yeah." He didn't want to talk about where he'd been. He needed to talk about where he was going, before common sense kicked in and prevented him from doing what he knew he needed to do. "Look, that part doesn't matter. I bought a ranch and there's a house on it, ready to be moved into." Damn it, she wasn't following him. He could see it in her eyes.

"What I'm trying to say is that I think, taking everything into consideration, it'd be best if we got married."

For the second time in the space of an hour, Lacy felt her jaw slacken and her mouth drop open.

CHAPTER FIVE

"BEST," Lacy repeated slowly, finally getting the use of her tongue back.

"Well, yeah." Uncomfortable, Connor wasn't sure if she was agreeing with him or just echoing the word he'd used. "For Chase." He turned his back so that it shielded them from any prying eyes should someone come into the room looking for them. By his reckoning, it bought them a couple of seconds. Judging by the unreadable expression on her face, he had a feeling he was going to need them. "He's got a right to grow up in something besides one room in a boarding house."

Something set to flower within her withered. "And that's why you want to marry me? To give Chase more rooms to grow up in?"

Her voice was low, hardly above a whisper, as numbness temporarily took her newfound strength away.

He didn't want her.

Well, what did she expect? her mind mocked. How many different ways did she need to be told, to be shown that Connor didn't love her—would never love her? She had to focus on what was important here. Her feelings couldn't take priority. At least Connor was a decent man who cared about the welfare of his son and wanted to take care of not only his son, but his son's mother, too. At the very least, she could have been excluded from the package.

It wasn't enough.

She said the word she never thought she would in response to a proposal from Connor. It was the most difficult word she'd ever uttered.

"No."

Astonished, he could only stare at her. The foundations for all his plans threatened to break apart, like plastic bricks left out too many days in the hot sun.

Maybe he'd heard wrong. "No?"

Her throat felt dry. The word crawled out again, sharp and scratchy. "No." She drew in a deep breath, feeling as if she was choking. "No, I won't marry you, Connor. Not to get real estate." Did he think so little of her that he'd imagine she'd sell herself so cheaply? She didn't need him for money. She needed him for many reasons, but money was not one of them. "And you don't have to worry about Chase being trapped in one room." A hint of sarcasm infiltrated her voice, though she hadn't meant it to. "By the time he notices the difference, I'll be earning enough to rent an apartment. Maybe even a small house. Shelby said I'm bringing them in at the diner. I'm sure that in time—''

Damn it, why couldn't she just say yes instead of giving him grief? He was trying to do the right thing here. ''There's no need to wait for time—''

She drew herself up to her full height, her eyes meeting his. It suddenly occurred to him that she would make a worthy opponent, if it came to that. The woman was not the shy, retiring violet she'd been when she left his house. A vague stirring of admiration began to poke its way forward.

''There is for me.''

Still, there was a small boy's life at stake here. ''Maybe you shouldn't be thinking just about you. Maybe you should think about Chase.'' He looked at her pointedly. Under no circumstances did he want her to know that he found her more attractive than ever. That if he wasn't so damn honorable, he'd give in to feelings that were circling him like hungry vultures, waiting for a break in his vigilance. ''I am.''

She would have felt the slap no less hard if he'd actually used his hand. ''Right. And you're making a magnificent sacrifice, tying yourself to me just to make certain your son has a decent place to live.''

Damn it, she was putting words into his mouth. ''Lacy, it's not like that.''

She raised her chin pugnaciously, daring him to prove her wrong. ''No? Then tell me what it's like, Connor. Please, tell me what it's like. Is it horrible, like having needles stuck in your eyes, or just unpleasant, like the sound of a dentist's drill starting up near you?''

He knew where she was going with this. Frustrated because he wanted to touch her no matter what his common sense told him, Connor shoved his hands into his pockets.

''Lacy, we've been all through this. I won't—I can't let myself have any feelings for you. Look what happened the last time.''

Did he have any idea how hurtful he was being? Only anger kept her tears back. ''Right. Disaster. Chase was conceived.''

Now that he'd seen him, held him, he didn't consider the conception of his son a disaster, not for him. But the timing left a great deal to be desired, especially for Lacy.

''And your whole life was turned upside down,'' he added.

It had been, when she'd been handed that letter and the envelope with severance pay that Janelle had said came from Connor. But that, too, she realized, had been part of Janelle's plan. It was behind her now that the truth was finally coming out. ''That was partly Janelle's doing. We both know that now.''

He blocked out the other woman's name, wishing he could have blocked out her existence, as well. The less he thought about the harm she could have inflicted on all their lives, the better. There was no point in going over the past, only the future. And his couldn't be the way he would have wanted it to be had he been irresponsible. "Lacy, I'm too old for you—"

"Oh, right." Excuses. The same flimsy excuses he'd given her before. The morning after they'd made love that first and only time. "One foot in the grave—I forgot."

Turning away so he wouldn't see the tears that were forming in her eyes, Lacy dragged her hand through her hair. What was she doing? Begging him to love her? She knew he didn't. Even now, he was saying he couldn't. All the reasons in the world wouldn't change his feelings if he had any for her. But he didn't. What he had was a sense of ethics. He was just being responsible.

The Maitlands were powerful people. What if he decided to use their power to take her to court and legally take Chase away from her? She liked the Maitlands, and they seemed to like her, but Connor and Chase were their blood. She was just the woman on the outside. She couldn't risk losing her baby yet again.

Besides, she did intend to remain in Austin so that Chase could have what she'd never had—a large extended family who cared for him.

This was, she supposed, the best possible deal she could be offered. But she couldn't accept it as it was. It needed some modifications.

Her back still to him, she gave him his answer. "I won't marry you."

The answer stung. And then Connor realized that she was crying. He could tell by the set of her shoulders, and he longed to take her into his arms, to wipe away the tears he knew had to be staining her cheeks. But that would be starting something he couldn't allow himself to finish.

"Lacy—"

Quickly wiping away the errant tears that had escaped with the heel of her hand, Lacy turned to look at him. Her head was held high, partly to impede the flow of tears, partly to put on a brave front.

She continued as if Connor hadn't interrupted. "But there's no reason to punish Chase and deny him things that he's entitled to just because you and I don't love each other."

She didn't love him.

This was what he wanted, to be assured that there were no emotional ties between them, not even a glimmer.

So why did it hurt to hear her reiterate exactly what he'd just mouthed? Why did his heart feel as if someone had stuck a hot branding iron across it, burning in a large, gaping hole instead of an insignia?

His eyes pinned her to the wall. "What are you saying?"

She told him as simply as possible. "That Chase and I will move in with you—as long as you give me a job.'' That was her condition. She had to earn her own way. He owed things to Chase, a multitude of things. He owed her only respect.

''A job?''

''Yes.'' Thoughts fell together as she spoke. ''The same one I had with you before would be appropriate, I think.'' With effort, she kept her voice light, as if she was merely discussing contract negotiations, not her future. ''Besides, cooking is something we both know I'm good at, even when someone bashes me in the head and I forget everything else. If you'd like, I can also keep house—''

He didn't want her waiting on him, didn't want her feeling like an employee. Whatever else, she wasn't that. Not any longer. ''Lacy—''

Deliberately, she ignored the protest in his voice. ''Although I'll expect more money for that. A housekeeper should be paid more than a mere cook.''

There was no talking her out of it. He could tell by the set of her jaw that she was stubbornly determined to do it her way. And maybe, in a way, he was relieved. If Lacy were his wife, even in name only, he might be tempted, sorely tempted, to make love with her again. To make the title a reality. Maybe he could hold out for a while, but not forever. Not when she looked at him like that.

He'd already promised himself not to compound one mistake with another. If they weren't married, not touching her would be easier.

Or so he told himself.

"Don't worry about the money," he told her, doling out his words slowly. "You'll be well taken care of."

But not the way she wanted to be, Lacy thought, unhappiness welling inside her. Grasping at her hurt and turning it into something she could work with, she cloaked herself in bravado.

"Yes, you always were a generous man." She tossed her hair over her shoulder and thrust out her hand. This was a business deal, pure and simple. "All right, it's official. I now pronounce us man and cook."

Connor found his hand surrounding hers.

He had no idea what possessed him. He was home free, or almost there. She was giving him what he wanted without his having to give up anything. It should have been all right.

Maybe it was the press of her hand against his. Maybe it was the scent of her perfume, softly, delicately swirling around his senses, infiltrating them like silent militia creeping lightly into enemy territory in the middle of the night.

Or maybe, somewhere in his iron heart, he had carried around the feel of her lips for almost two years.

Whatever the reason, Connor found himself pulling Lacy closer to him than he should have, their hands still joined.

The next moment, it was their lips that were joined, as well, and a flood of all those feelings he told himself were firmly under control suddenly washed over him. Drenching him. Snatching his breath away.

For the briefest of moments, without thinking of any of the consequences, Connor discovered himself hungrily getting lost in what he had remembered so vividly despite all his efforts not to. Her kiss, all sweetness and giving, undid him. Made him wish with all his heart that there weren't a score of years separating them. That he was free to be as young as she made his heart feel.

He didn't want to want her.

But he did.

Lacy wanted to push him away. She wanted to drag him closer. She wanted this to go on forever, to be her reality and all the words he'd just said to the contrary to be the fantasy, the make-believe, instead of the other way around.

Most of all, Lacy realized, she wanted not to be at his mercy like this.

By all rights, she should shout at him and run away, negating any agreements just made. Severing all ties and fleeing with her child before she sacrificed her mind all over again, this time to a man who held her very soul in the palm of his hand. Held it there and didn't give a damn that he had the power to do so.

But Lacy remained where she was, feet firmly planted on the ground, savoring this because she knew it might not happen again and she needed it. Needed it more than the food on her plate or the air she breathed.

She knew that made her weak. Somehow, she couldn't bring herself to care. Not about that. Not yet.

With a soft sigh, she leaned into him, her fingers tangling in his hair, her soul tangling in the moment. The kiss deepened, threatening to take her under for the third time.

"Are congratulations in order?"

The voice wedged its way into the moment and brought reality, cold and hard, with it. Lacy felt the pang instantly. Connor had already jerked back from her. She tossed her head, making damn sure her eyes looked as if they were sparkling.

She stared straight at Jake. "Yes. Connor has just asked me to be his cook, and I've accepted."

"Cook?" Jake damn well never saw anyone kiss their cook like that. Who did they think they were fooling? "Is that a euphemism?"

"No, that's a position," Lacy answered brightly. "A position I can fill very capably, luckily for Connor."

And then the full ramifications of what she was doing hit her. She caught her lip between her teeth, her eyes slanting toward Connor. She felt partially vindicated in that he didn't look as if he were exactly capable of doing long division in his head at the moment. At least she wasn't the only one affected by what had just happened.

"But that means I'm going to have to tell Shelby I'm leaving. Unless, of course," she said to Connor, "you don't mind having all your meals served either very, very early or very, very late."

Why did she insist on going on with this charade? "I already told you," Connor told her impatiently, "you won't have to worry about money—"

"Um, I think maybe I hear Camille calling for me upstairs," Jake murmured. Part of being able to survive as long as he had with his skin intact was knowing to get out before things heated up too much. And there was definitely heat here.

Didn't Connor understand? Lacy thought, exasperated. "I wasn't thinking about money, I was thinking about loyalty. That's far more important."

Connor failed to see the problem. "Shelby can find someone else to do the cooking at the diner. She did before."

He made it sound as if she was completely expendable. As if anyone could easily fill her shoes. Did he really feel that way? "She says my cooking is what was bringing customers in." Having given her word to Connor, she could not turn back. Lacy sighed. "But a deal's a deal." And then an idea surfaced. "Maybe I can still make the pies for her and send them in. You wouldn't mind your cook being a little enterprising on her own, would you?''

He refused to get pulled into this. It was safer to remain on the outskirts. She'd come around soon enough and settle down, he promised himself. But the promise wasn't made with confidence. ''You can do what you want, Lacy. Your life's your own.''

He said it so cavalierly. She felt her back going up. ''But not my son's.''

Connor's eyes narrowed. ''No, not *our* son's.'' He purposely amended the reference, his eyes on hers. ''Chase's life is half mine until he's of legal age. Then it's all his.''

''I see.'' Inside, she felt as if she were trembling, whether with anger, anticipation or some other emotion she wasn't certain. She struggled to get it under control. ''So I guess this agreement of ours is for a little over seventeen years.'' She paused. ''It's a long time to sell your soul into slavery.'' And even longer to remain so close to a man who didn't love her. She wasn't sure if she was up to it.

Slavery? Where did she get these thoughts? ''Lacy, I just said—''

''I know what you said. And I know what you're thinking.'' That he would never love her, but that he was confident he had control over her.

That kiss had sealed her fate, and she damned him for it. There was no way she was ever going to love any other man, even if Connor didn't love her. And for that, she could almost hate him.

Her head began to ache as the complexity of the situation assaulted her.

She saw the uneasy look in his eyes. Maybe he wasn't quite as confident as she thought he was. It helped a little. "Don't worry, I won't go back on our agreement. Chase and I'll move into your place as soon as I talk to Shelby and make my arrangements."

The sigh that escaped him was one of relief. "All right, I can respect that."

Her eyes narrowed as she looked at him before returning to the dining room. "You have no choice in the matter, Mr. O'Hara."

Leaving him to follow or not, Lacy went straight for Chase, who was still sitting in his high chair. Megan was beside the baby, every inch the doting grandmother.

As Megan watched Lacy cross to her, she tried to discern what was on her mind from the young woman's expression. Lacy looked preoccupied. And perhaps a little troubled, as well.

"You know," Megan told her kindly as Lacy began to undo the straps that held Chase in his chair, "you don't have to go back to the boarding house tonight. Or ever, for that matter." She'd given it only cursory thought. That was all it took to make up her mind. "You're perfectly welcome to remain here for as long as you like.'' Her eyes smiled at Lacy. ''You're family now.''

Lacy wished she could really believe that. ''That's very generous of you, Mrs. Maitland.'' Lacy sensed that Connor was behind her. ''I guess I can see where Connor gets it from—even if he's not aware of it.''

Not quite following, Megan inclined her head. ''Gets what from?''

''His generosity of spirit.'' She wanted Connor's mother to know the exact circumstances that were involved. The last thing she needed was for the Maitlands to think she was living with Connor as his mistress. ''Connor has asked Chase and me to move in with him.''

''Oh?'' Megan's eyes shifted to Connor's face.

He didn't have the look about him of a man who'd just asked a woman to marry him. But maybe he hadn't. Lacy had said move in, not marry. Her gaze returned to Lacy, patiently waiting for clarification.

''Yes,'' Lacy told her, loving the way Chase snuggled against her. This was worth everything, she thought, even not getting on with her life. ''I'm going to be his cook—so he can have decent meals when he's not eating here,'' she added with a smile as she looked at Megan.

Megan heard the pain, however subtly veiled, within Lacy's voice. Unsure of what exactly was going on, she promised herself to get to the bottom of it as soon as she could. For now, she rested a hand on the young woman's shoulder.

"Are you sure this is what you want?"

That someone was actually concerned about her feelings touched Lacy. She wished with all her heart that Connor had grown up living with this woman instead of Clarise, who'd taught him how to seal himself off from everyone and everything. Maybe if he had grown up here, he would have used his heart for something other than an organ that kept his body functioning and going through the motions of being alive.

"I want," Lacy told her, offering the brightest smile she could, "whatever's best for Chase, and being close to his father is best."

Megan nodded, then surprised Lacy by pressing a kiss to her cheek. "I think I'm going to like you, Lacy. Very, very much."

For the moment, Lacy was left speechless. And properly appreciative.

CHAPTER SIX

"IT NEEDS WORK," Connor warned Lacy as he opened the front door to the new ranch house two days later. He watched her as she walked in, trying to gauge her thoughts by the expression on her face.

He got nowhere.

The ranch house was new only in the sense that it was new to him. It was probably close to eighty years old, at the very least, and if he had to guess, he would have said that the last repairs or additions had taken place thirty years ago. And that was being charitable.

One sweeping look around revealed that renovations were desperately needed. But the acreage was good and the proximity to his family better. Connor counted himself lucky to have found the ranch on such short notice.

"Doesn't everything?" Lacy countered vaguely, lost in thought.

Holding Chase to her, she looked around slowly. She made her way to the large bay window that faced the direction they'd just come from. The heavy, dust-laden drapes trapped any sunlight, keeping it from entering the room. She located the drapery cord and tugged at it. The drapes refused to budge. She took a corner of the dirty fabric and pulled hard. A little of the drape gave.

Sunlight struggled to get through windows that were almost opaque.

She'd been in better places, she mused. But she'd also been in worse. And with its high wood-beam ceilings and spacious living room, the place possessed definite possibilities. She always believed in looking positively at the possibilities.

Lacy crossed to the fireplace. The bricks were almost bowed beneath the thick layers of dirt, some crumbling in places. The fireplace, like the rest of the house, had the air of long-standing neglect.

Wrapping her arms around the baby, Lacy debated where best to start reviving the victim. She turned to look at Connor, wondering if it was her imagination or if he was watching her intently. Why? What did he expect her to say?

Lacy wandered over to a leather sofa. It was hard to say what the original color had been. Somewhere between black and tan.

Her mouth curved. She wondered if she would stick to the furniture if she sat down. ''Looks like housekeeping wasn't a high priority on the last owner's list.''

He gave her the pertinent information, spitting the words out like an old-fashioned teletype. ''Widower. Lived alone after his only son was killed in the Gulf

War. Garrett said he kind of let things slide after that.'' *Slide* wasn't the word she would have used, Lacy thought. More like a chicken hawk's spiraling descent. ''The man was just waiting for an offer. I gave him a fair price.''

''I'm sure you did.''

Probably more than fair, if she knew Connor. Lacy looked around again. She didn't see anywhere she'd be willing to put Chase down, so she continued holding him as she made her way around the first floor. Almost afraid to venture there, she saved the kitchen for last.

The stove was going to be the first thing to go, she decided the moment she saw the blackened appliance. She had her doubts it even functioned.

It was time to stop being a spectator and dive into the challenge. Lacy turned and almost bumped into Connor. He was standing behind her like a shadow. ''I think I've seen enough.''

Placing a protective hand over her son, she made her way out of the dreary room and into the living room. The space looked better to her now. It was all relative, she mused.

Lacy raised her eyes to his. ''Remember what I said about housekeeping being extra?''

He'd half expected her to declare that she couldn't live in a place like this. Connor had been prepared to argue the ranch's good points. Her reference to the other night and their agreement threw him for a second. He wasn't sure exactly what she was driving at, but he took a stab at it.

"I don't expect you to do any cleaning."

Maybe that was why she was so willing to do it. "I was going to say that the first week or so is on the house—probably along with everything else," she added under her breath. "At any rate, I can't have Chase living in a place like this."

"You're right."

What was he thinking, Connor upbraided himself, bringing Chase here? He didn't particularly care about conditions for himself. All he required was a strong cup of coffee in the morning and some kind of bed to fall into at night, and the last was negotiable. But it was different for a baby. A baby needed sanitary conditions.

"You and Chase can stay with Megan—my mother," he amended, though the word still didn't come easily to him, "until I can get a cleaning crew to come out here."

He missed her point, Lacy thought, beginning to slowly survey the room again. "I'm not about to impose on your mother a second longer than I already have. This is your ranch house so this is where Chase and I are going to stay." At the last second, she avoided walking into a spiderweb. Lacy shivered, backing away. "Minus the cobwebs, of course." She took a closer look at the intricate handiwork that spread from one edge of the fireplace to the opposite wall. "Lord, those spiders must be huge." She wasn't squeamish, but she sincerely hoped she wouldn't run into the spider that had made this particular web. It was probably as big as a hummingbird. "I don't suppose you've got any cleaning products here."

He'd had the electricity turned on, and there were a few provisions in the pantry, but he hadn't thought any further than that. He'd had his mind more on the kind of ranch he'd wanted this to be—a horse ranch—than on the house.

Connor shoved his hands into his pockets, shrugging. "Well, I—"

The somewhat sheepish tone gave her all the answer she needed.

"That's what I thought." Mentally, she began making a list of things they were going to need immediately to make the house even vaguely livable. She saw the surprise on his face when she put out her hand. "I'd like the keys to the pickup, please."

He took them out of his pocket and placed them in the palm of her hand. "Planning on going into town to stock up?"

She closed her hand over the keys. "Yes."

"And what are you planning to use for money?"

She'd forgotten about that. It rankled her to ask, but this wasn't the time for pride. Besides, this was his place, not hers. Shifting Chase slightly, she put out her hand a second time and looked at Connor expectantly. "I was hoping you'd solve that by giving me your credit card—or a large wad of cash."

He dug into his wallet, extracting several hundred-dollar bills. He didn't believe in using credit cards, but he supposed he was going to have to develop the knack eventually. A man could only hold out against progress so long.

He didn't bother counting, but handed her the wad. "Just what is it you intend on getting?"

Pausing at the door, Lacy looked over her shoulder. The smile she gave him just before she left with Chase went right through him, clear down to the bone.

"Everything."

As far back as he could remember, he'd always been an early riser. Living on a working ranch had made that a necessity from the time he was old enough to pitch in. He'd enjoyed being part of the process, even though Clarise had insisted that he refrain, letting the hired hands do the work. But he had refused, immersing himself in the tasks that made a ranch a successful enterprise instead of just so much territory bordered by fences.

Getting up earlier than the sun had been something he took for granted. Most of the time, he was the first one to see the dawn.

But this morning, in this brand-new old place, someone had beat him to it. He realized he'd woken up listening to a distant, not completely identifiable sound. For the time being, he'd taken the bedroom on the first floor, insisting that Lacy and Chase have the master suite until accommodations could be readied for them. The room that would be used as a nursery was crowded with broken furniture and a lifetime accumulation of things that could be charitably referred to as memorabilia. Connor called it junk.

He slipped into the clothes he'd worn the day before. He'd change into a clean set after his shower. The first order of business was to see what that noise was and to make himself one hell of a strong cup of coffee. He had a feeling he was going to need it.

He found both coffee—already made—and the source of the noise in the same place. The living room. Lacy, wearing an old shirt and shorts, her hair tied back and partially hidden under a red bandanna, was in the middle of trying to remove more than ten years' worth of dirt and grime from what appeared to have once been a pristine white and gray flagstone fireplace.

Chase, sitting on his well-padded bottom in the playpen she'd set up in the middle of the room, was busy entertaining himself with an array of colorful plastic blocks spread out in front of him. He was babbling away, as if he were telling himself jokes.

"You look like Cinderella," Connor heard himself commenting.

She glanced over her shoulder, not surprised to see

him there. She'd felt his presence the moment he'd looked in the doorway. She supposed that was both her gift and her curse.

"I could use a few dozen helpful mice right around now," she confessed. She'd been working awhile, beginning immediately after she'd fed Chase. She nodded at the coffee table in front of the sofa. There was a fresh pot of coffee plugged in. It minimized trips to the kitchen. "Help yourself to coffee. It'll get your blood going."

Looking at her already accomplished that, he thought. But he nodded and made his way to the table. "Thanks."

Connor waited until the long drag of the dark brew he swallowed kicked in. Then he looked at what she was doing. The sofa had a vague color to it, as did the coffee table. Both were functional but sported more than their share of cracks.

The fireplace looked like a perfect study of before and after, half of it dark white and the other half a sooty combination of black and grit. She was working too hard.

He knew she didn't seem to mind, but he did. He hadn't agreed to this arrangement to turn her into a slave.

"I told you that you didn't have to do that." He took another long swallow. "That I'd get a crew out."

He'd had a very vocal discussion with her about

that yesterday. He'd relented about the kitchen only because he'd been afraid of a grease fire starting when she made dinner if she'd left it the way it was. He'd gone to make phone calls and been amazed at the difference when he'd returned. The woman was clearly a wonder.

Lacy shrugged away his protest. "I was up early. Besides, cleaning gives me a feeling of renewal."

He laughed shortly under his breath and took another long sip of coffee. "Then this place'll have you positively reborn."

Feeling somewhat useless, Connor sat on the sofa. The newly cleaned, cracked dark tan leather sighed as it accepted his weight. He had a feeling a few tears had just widened under him. For a few minutes, Connor did nothing but drink his coffee and watch Lacy. She worked tirelessly.

And made him feel guilty.

He started to mentally review their arrangement and found it lacking all over again. Maybe now that she'd had some time to think it over, she had changed her mind. It was worth broaching. "You know, people might talk."

Wiping her forehead with the back of her hand, Lacy paused to look at him, surprised at the sentence fragment that seemed to come out of nowhere. He'd been so quiet, if he'd been anyone other than Connor, she would have forgotten he was there.

"About?"

Why was she making him repeat himself? She knew damn well what he was referring to. "About the fact that you're a young woman, living in a man's house. The father of your child's house and, well..." Delicately, for her sake, he trailed off.

Getting on her knees, she started working on another section of the fireplace. It was really coming around, she congratulated herself. Too bad the same couldn't be said of Connor.

But Connor, she reminded herself, was a lost cause. "Since when do you care what people say?"

"I don't." He never had, never would. But he wasn't thinking of himself right now. "But I thought you might." Their eyes met and held for a moment. "That it might bother you because what they say could someday reach Chase."

With any luck, she would raise her son to have thicker skin than she'd had. Humor curved her mouth. "We've got a few weeks before Chase starts listening to mindless gossip."

He was being serious and she was making a joke out of it. Annoyed, Connor set his cup down harder than he should have on the table. The sound reverberated through the room. Chase looked at him with huge eyes before he went back to squeezing the blocks between his chubby hands.

"Damn it, Lacy, a woman's reputation isn't something to be so lightly regarded, no matter what those damn magazines say about equality." Frustrated, he dragged his hand through his hair. "Hell, when push comes to shove, men value their reputations, too."

Lacy wasn't thinking about reputations. She couldn't control what people said. She could only exercise control over herself—and pray she had some sort of influence over the ones she loved. Like Connor. "How about their hearts, Connor? Do they value their hearts?"

Now what was she driving at? Annoyed, Connor poured himself a second cup of coffee, just as dark, just as inky as the first. "What?"

She went on as if he hadn't interrupted. "Because I value mine, and when I stand before God and preacher and say those words that I'm only going to say once, it's going to be to a man I love who loves me back, not because of what someone's Aunt Gertie whispers to someone else's Aunt Selma behind the canned peas display in the local grocery store."

Well, she'd certainly made her feelings clear, Connor thought. "Supermarket," he corrected, a small smile curving his mouth. "They've got supermarkets here, not grocery stores."

"They've also got better things to do than talk about the living arrangements chosen by one better-than-average cook."

She was a hell of a lot better than better-than-average, but he wasn't about to let himself get sidetracked by correcting her. There were bigger things at stake than a mere compliment.

"I'm a Maitland now." On his feet, restless, Connor shoved his hands into his pockets. "Like it or not, that makes my life everyone's business." He looked at her. "And you're in my life, Lacy."

She wished she could hear an iota of happiness at the turn of events. To give him his due, he didn't make it sound as if it was a plague, either. But she wanted more. She wanted him to want her in his life. "Only in the most cursory fashion."

He wanted to say something to negate her statement. To let her know—again—why he'd chosen to do what he had. And why he couldn't let himself love her. The crucial word here was *couldn't*. Because he could love her. So very easily. He could let down the barriers he'd erected around his heart and let himself love her. There was so much within her to love. The sweetness, the innocent purity that reminded him the world wasn't all dark and forbidding. Wasn't all shrouded in secrets for its own gain. Lacy had never wanted anything from him but his heart.

But it was for her that he refused to let it happen. For her sake he kept himself in check. She needed someone vital, someone who could keep up with her. Someone she wouldn't have to take care of someday while she was still young.

"My point exactly," he finally said. "I don't want you tainted. But I'm still willing to go through with it, Lacy."

Go through with it. He made it sound like he was

facing a firing squad. Didn't he see why she couldn't accept? Why, even when it would grant her exactly what she wanted, to be Mrs. Connor O'Hara, she couldn't "go through with it"?

"For the sake of my reputation," she said quietly.

He had the eeriest feeling that he was a man facing the calm before the storm. "For the sake of your reputation."

It took effort to bank down the sudden flare of anger she felt. Picking up the rag, she began cleaning again. Furiously. "Don't trouble yourself. I can take care of my reputation just fine, thank you."

Maybe what was stopping Lacy from agreeing was that she thought he'd stand in her way, expect things from her. "You could still come and go as you please, if that's what's worrying you. As long as you're discreet, there's no reason—"

She doubted if she'd ever been so insulted in her life. Did he think she'd been some kind of mindless floozy the night she made love with him? That she could just carelessly go from man to man while the son she'd borne slept peacefully at home with the man she'd created him with?

"I think you should stop right there," she warned him through lips that barely moved. "I wouldn't go on if I were you. Not while I've got sharp tools within my reach."

Why was she getting so incensed? "I'm only thinking of you."

But not in the right way, she thought. She kept her back to him. "Do us both a favor and start thinking of yourself for a while. Like I said, I can take care of myself."

He was beginning to believe that she could. Connor regarded her in silence for a long moment. "Just when did you develop this independent streak?"

She raised her eyes to his. "It was there all along. You just didn't notice."

"I guess not." Uncomfortable, he let the matter go and looked around. It was a big room. Lacy couldn't be left to tackle it all by herself. "Anything you want me to do?"

Yes, damn you, love me so I don't feel like such a fool loving you.

She shrugged indifferently. "Can't think of a thing. Why don't you go to your room and get properly dressed? I'll have breakfast ready when you come back out."

He looked at what he was wearing. "What makes you think I'm not properly dressed?"

"You're wearing the same thing you were wearing yesterday. I don't ever remember you doing that," she said offhandedly.

Connor shrugged. "Maybe a shower'll make me feel more human, at that."

"Make it a quick one," she warned. "The hot water runs out after about three minutes. I learned the hard way. My whole body turned into one large goose bump because I couldn't rinse off fast enough.''

"Thanks for the warning.'' He tried not to let the image she'd just described linger in his mind as he walked out of the room.

He had absolutely no success.

At the very least, he mused philosophically, come winter, this would definitely help him save on the heating bill.

CHAPTER SEVEN

SETTING a cup of coffee down, Connor settled at his desk in the room he'd taken over as his den. The sun was at his back, peering intently into the room like an odd man out kibitzing at a bridge table. Lacy had worked her magic in here. It didn't look like the same room he'd first seen. For that matter, it didn't look like the same house.

In a little more than three short weeks, like a tireless whirlwind, Lacy had methodically worked her way from room to room, renovating, repairing, restoring. A new house, he thought, and a new Lacy.

Leaning back in the newly refinished chair, he closed his eyes and let the sun warm him.

The Lacy he remembered had been retiring, shy. Innocent. That had been part of the reason he'd felt so damned guilty the morning after he'd woken up to find her in his bed. To find that he had made love with her and that he had been her first.

The first man in a woman's life should be special, especially if that woman was Lacy. That left him out of the running. He was old enough to be her father, albeit, he amended with a fleeting touch of amusement, a young father, but still a father. There were twenty years separating them.

He'd had no business being the one who'd taken away her virginity. No business at all. Even if it had been the sweetest, most memorable occasion in his life.

She had been eager to please, he recalled. Eager to be with him and experience all the mysteries that existed between a man and a woman. But on the whole he had to admit the word that best described her was sweet.

While still sweet, the new Lacy had a punch to her. A pizzazz the old Lacy had been missing. There was determination in her eyes and independence in her bearing. He just had to be in the same room with her to feel it.

Connor had to admit that the new improved Lacy intrigued him as much as the old Lacy had attracted him. Maybe even more, because he liked women who held their own, women who didn't attach themselves to a man like some sort of clinging vine.

This Lacy was confident. She could stand on her own if she needed to. *Did* stand on her own, he corrected, remembering with a bittersweet pang the way she'd turned down his proposal. The old Lacy, he was certain, would have eagerly jumped on it, accepting faster than she could draw the next breath.

In a way, he rather missed the old Lacy.

Connor frowned. He wasn't making any sense.

With a sigh, he dragged a hand through his unruly hair.

New or old, Lacy wasn't his to ponder over. She couldn't be. If she still appeared to care about him, it was because she lacked a father figure in her life. Eventually, she would get over that and realize that what she wanted was a husband, not a father. What would he do, after giving her his heart, if she walked away, a polite apology on her lips? Lacy could begin again, but he would be left with the ashes of a failed relationship and no inclination to reinvent himself.

It was better this way.

Better to pretend that the scent of her perfume, clinging to every damn surface in the house, didn't infiltrate his senses and drive him crazy. Better to pretend that he didn't think of her at the oddest times of the day. Yesterday, it had happened while he'd been at the horse auction.

Horses had always been his passion, and he wanted to make this new ranch work—as only a man who was suddenly desperate to emerge in his own light wanted something to work. He might now be part of the Maitland dynasty, but he was his own man. And he needed to make his own success, not just sail along on the coattails of relatives he hadn't even known he had.

But still, in the middle of a heated bidding war, he'd suddenly envisioned the way she'd looked early one morning when he'd happened upon her unexpectedly, the sun filtering through the almost gauze-like cotton blouse she'd had on, giving him more than an eyeful of the firm, supple body beneath. Their night of lovemaking came barreling down the runway of his mind back to him.

He'd lost the horse to another bidder. And had sacrificed his self-respect. He didn't know what was wrong with him. He'd always had more control over his thoughts than that.

Connor looked at the pen on his desk. He hadn't even picked it up. He'd risen early with the intention of getting through the ponderous paperwork that was beginning to pile up on his desk, but he couldn't seem to get his head together.

The baby was crying again. Connor's frown deepened. It seemed to him that Chase had been doing a lot of crying since last night. Lacy hadn't been down to breakfast when he'd walked into the kitchen, something that struck him as odd. She'd been up before him every morning since they'd entered this arrangement.

He wondered if something was wrong.

For one thing, Lacy didn't let Chase cry. She would stop whatever she was doing and pick the baby up when he seemed upset or uncomfortable.

The crying became louder.

Something had to be wrong. Connor pushed his chair back, stood and walked into the hall. A hall that was well lit instead of being obscured in semi-darkness the way it had been when he'd bought the place. One of the first things Lacy had done was insist that he get ceiling light fixtures. The next thing he knew, he had light fixtures on the floor and his half brother Jake on a ladder, installing the new lights for him. Jake had grinned at him and said his past work with the FBI had taught him a thing or two about wiring.

Connor made his way down the hall, following the sound of Chase's cries. It wasn't easy getting used to that, to having people volunteering their services, poking themselves into his life when he hadn't asked them to. Not that he ever would have. It wasn't his way. The background he'd had was one of reserve. You didn't ask for help. You did it yourself or it didn't get done. This family network was going to take a hell of a lot of getting used to.

The door to the room Lacy shared with Chase was open. Her latest undertaking, the bedroom, was a work in progress with tools, fabric and things he wouldn't even attempt to identify scattered on the floor.

Connor picked his way slowly, not wanting to step on anything. Baby in her arms, Lacy seemed oblivious to his presence. Wearing paint-splattered jeans and the baggy T-shirt he'd gotten used to seeing her in, she had the look of someone who hadn't slept in the last twenty-four hours.

"What's the matter?"

Her head jerked in his direction. "Oh, Connor, sorry, I didn't hear you come in. I'm sorry if Chase disturbed you."

The apology irritated him. Did she think he was some kind of heartless ogre, there to complain about a baby's cries when it was so obvious that Chase was distressed? But because she looked tired, Connor refrained from saying anything, shrugging away her words instead.

"I was just going over bills. I could stand a little disturbing." He came closer to her, looking at Chase. Still wearing his bright blue sleeper with the feet, the little boy seemed as oblivious to him as his mother had been. "What's wrong with him?"

She wondered if that was an impatient question because Chase had disturbed him, or if it was an intuitive one because he sensed something was wrong with the little boy. Looking at Connor, she didn't see the mark of impatience on his face and gave him the benefit of the doubt. It was a habit.

Lacy passed her hand over the small forehead, brushing back the damp hair. "He's running a little fever and—"

"A fever?" Connor looked from her to the baby. Somewhere inside him, a small alarm went off. "Is that normal?"

"Only when you're sick," she said wearily. "I think he picked up a cold."

The words came out before he could think better

of them. "Small wonder, the way you drag him around with you wherever you go." She was always driving off to one place or another, looking for more things for the house. Chase went with her, strapped into his car seat.

Exhausted, with more than a touch of guilt, Lacy felt her temper flare. "Coddling him would only be worse." She pressed her lips together, knowing that had come out too sharply. She softened her voice. "He has to build up an immunity."

He wasn't about to debate this with her. What mattered now was Chase. "How long has he been like this?"

Despite the situation, she smiled. Seeing Connor reduced to a worried parent helped her deal with her growing concerns about Chase's condition.

"Not long. Just since late yesterday afternoon." She tried to placate both his worries and her own. "You have to remember that a baby's temperature can go up and down a great deal even during the course of a single day."

He had absolutely no idea about temperatures or anything else that went with raising a child. The fact that he didn't made Connor feel inadequate. It was all Greek to him.

"How do you know that?"

As she talked, she continued to walk the floor, rubbing Chase's back, hoping the constant motion would soothe him. "Tons and tons of baby-care books I've read. The second I found out I was pregnant, I began reading everything I could find on the subject of babies.''

After the initial shock and fear had settled into something manageable and she'd made peace with what was happening in her life, Lacy had been determined not to float ignorantly along through this adventure called motherhood. Nor did she want to be one of those alarmist mothers who ran to the doctor at the slightest sign of a problem, only to be embarrassed because she'd overreacted.

Connor might know nothing about raising children, but he was pretty attuned to the sounds of distress. He'd always known when one of his horses needed attention, and a baby wasn't all that different from a colt. Coming around behind her, Connor peered at the small, flushed face nestled against Lacy's shoulder.

''He doesn't sound as if he's read the same books. Here, let me take him.'' Not waiting for an argument, he slipped his hands around Chase's small body and took him into his arms. The baby definitely felt warmer than Connor thought he should. He glanced at Lacy. ''You look exhausted. Have you been getting any sleep lately?''

She vaguely remembered lying face down on the bed for a few minutes or so sometime during the night when Chase had drifted off to sleep for a bit. ''Enough.''

He arched a brow. "How many hours is enough?"

"Try minutes," she corrected, a bemused smile on her lips. Did he really care, or was he just worried that she might turn into a liability? "Four or five."

He looked at her as if she'd just announced that she was about to climb Mount McKinley naked in the middle of January. "Look, if you get sick," he said sternly, "I can't take care of both of you."

She was right, she thought. He was afraid she'd turn into a burden. "No one asked you to, and I won't get sick." Lacy began to take Chase from him and was surprised when Connor turned his body away, preventing her from getting a good hold.

Chase's whimpering turned into a wail. Without thinking, Connor began to imitate the motion he'd seen her using and rubbed Chase's back. "Oh, you have a guarantee for that, do you?"

Watching him, she couldn't keep the smile back. Maybe there was hope for the man yet. "You know, anyone listening to you would say you cared."

He wasn't comfortable talking about his feelings. Hell, he wasn't even comfortable feeling his feelings. "Sure I care," he grumbled. "You get sick, I get left with more work on my hands."

She laughed softly, shaking her head. "You do know how to turn a girl's head."

The thought of her getting sick and leaving him to cope on his own with Chase scared the hell out of him. He didn't let himself go there. "I wasn't thinking of turning your head so much as wringing your neck," he muttered.

Well, that certainly sounded more like Connor. Lacy raised her eyes innocently to his. "A new cure for colds?"

"Pretty much for everything that ails you," he retorted dryly. "You know, he does feel pretty hot. I think we should take him to the doctor."

She noticed that he said *we* instead of saying she should take the baby herself. *You're a lot softer than you'd like people to think, Connor O'Hara, no matter how much you bark.*

Lacy nodded. "Your mother's had him getting regular checkups with Ford." Turning, she opened a bureau drawer and took out fresh clothes for Chase. "As a matter of fact, I was just about to call the office to ask if I could bring Chase in."

She took a fresh diaper from the pack she kept in the corner, then placed the clothes and diaper on the bed. She smiled at the unhappy baby as she took him from Connor. Chase felt hotter than he had a few minutes ago. "Hang on, little guy," she said. "Mommy and Daddy are going to get you some relief."

"I'll be outside," Connor muttered, backing out of the room.

Mommy and Daddy. The words echoed in his head. They were a set now, if not a couple. That one tiny human being had forever bonded him to Lacy.

No matter how far off the beaten path he wandered in his life, there was that single truth to guide him home. He'd made a child with Lacy. A living, breathing testimony to the fact that he had passed this way.

It was, he realized, a little humbling.

FORD CARRINGTON paused to write a few notes on the freshly made up chart in his hands. "Just a slight case of otitis media," he assured Connor and Lacy without looking up.

It had been a busy morning, more so than usual. His waiting room was packed, but Ford had found a way to squeeze the child in to be seen ahead of the others. This was, after all, the founder's grandson. Certain shortcuts could be taken and forgiven.

The examination over, Lacy began to slip Chase's shirt on. They had breezed right through the waiting room and into an examination room as soon as she had given the nurse behind the counter their name. She knew that was taking unfair advantage of Connor's connections, but when it came to Chase, she had to admit she could be a little less than fair. She didn't want the baby sitting in the waiting room when he was so obviously miserable and where he was susceptible to catching even more germs than he already had.

"English, Ford," Connor urged, trying unsuccessfully to mask his irritation. "Tell me what's wrong with Chase in English."

Taking the stethoscope from around his neck and tucking a portion of it into his lab coat pocket, Ford smiled at Connor's impatience. It wasn't anything he wasn't accustomed to.

"It's an inner ear infection, Connor. Very common in kids." He took out his prescription pad, wrote something then signed it. Ford tore it off and held the paper out to Connor. "Have this filled either here or at your local drugstore, and he should be good as new in about a week."

Connor stared at the strange, unintelligible markings on the paper, then folded it. "A week? Isn't that a long time for him to suffer?"

Yes, the scales were definitely tipping in the man's favor, Ford thought. "He won't be suffering during that week, Connor." He tapped the paper Connor held. "That's what the medicine is for. Amoxicillin, one teaspoon, three times a day," Ford instructed. He looked from Connor to Lacy. They made a rather nice pair. Certainly made a handsome baby between them. "People tell me it gets easier after you've had a few," he promised.

"Uh-huh," Connor grunted. He saw no reason to tell the young doctor that he had no intentions of having a few more. That Chase had been a completely, unexpected surprise and that if he hadn't been overcome with grief and a few too many drinks to anesthetize the pain, the boy would have never happened. It was none of the pediatrician's business.

"Just make sure he takes this three times a day," Ford repeated to Lacy. "And keep the bottle in the refrigerator."

Connor wasn't entirely convinced that the doctor was being as thorough as he should. "There's no chance of this being anything else, is there?"

At the door, Ford paused. "Something else? Like what?"

Connor was out of his depth here and he knew it. Still, this was his son. He shoved his hands deep into his pockets. "Well, I've heard the new strains of flu are particularly hard on little kids."

Ford suppressed a weary sigh. "The flu season is generally in winter, but it never hurts to be vigilant. You can call me any time if he develops other symptoms. But for now, this is just a middle ear infection."

Ford opened the door and stepped out for a moment. When he returned, he was holding a sterile wrapped syringe in his hand.

Connor had thought the visit over. He eyed the instrument in Ford's hand. "What's that?"

Ford smiled reassuringly. "I'm going to give Chase a shot to get him on his way." Taking off the wrapper, he held the syringe up, expelling any air.

Connor'd always hated needles. "To what? Pain?"

"No, the medicine acts faster if it's released directly into the bloodstream. This is to lower his fever." He looked at Lacy. "Hold him very still, please. This is going into the fatty tissue in his leg. It'll hurt less that way."

Chase howled as the needle went in. Holding him, Lacy winced, swearing she could feel the injection right along with her son. She glanced at Connor to see his reaction and saw him flinch, as well.

Despite her concern and the situation, Lacy felt something warm wrap around her heart.

CHAPTER EIGHT

GETTING OFF the elevator, Connor looked around, scanning the first floor. Like some others of his species, he loathed asking directions.

Chase was beginning to doze off against Lacy's shoulder. She shifted to get a better view of Connor. "What are you looking for?"

"The pharmacy. I want to get this prescription filled as soon as possible and I haven't the vaguest idea where the closest one to the ranch is."

She had a suspicion that he didn't know where any were in the area, even though he'd been in Austin several months. Connor's approach to life was to assimilate information as he needed it. The one exception was horses. Everything else was left in the shadows.

"Everything else," she knew, included her, as well, but she'd made her peace with that.

Or was trying to.

"The doctor said it was to the left of the elevator, in the opposite direction of the entrance," she reminded him softly.

"Right." He should have remembered that. But

he'd been so concerned about Chase, so worried as he watched the needle sink into his soft flesh that he'd only half heard the pediatrician. It wasn't like him. He usually could remain detached, distant from whatever was happening. But then, a man couldn't be faulted for being somewhat confused, having gone through what he had in the last few months. Discovering that his world, his childhood had been a tissue of lies.

Anyone would be a little off kilter after that, Connor reasoned, at least for a while.

The trouble was he was a lot off kilter and he didn't like it.

He glanced at Chase. "Is he asleep?"

"Looks that way," she murmured as she walked beside Connor. Lacy couldn't resist pressing a soft kiss to the top of the baby's head. He felt cooler already. Or maybe it was just wishful thinking. "Poor little guy's tuckered out."

Connor nodded, not knowing what to say. Afraid that anything he said might give away his feelings. Instead, he glanced at the piece of paper in his hand. "Hope this doesn't take long."

Lacy wondered if that meant he had somewhere else to be.

LESS THAN TEN minutes later, Chase's medicine was safely tucked into a small white paper bag with the hospital's logo on the side and they were on their way out.

"Well, that was quick," Lacy said, one eye on Chase as she followed Connor. Her arms tightened around the baby. She wanted him to get as much uninterrupted sleep as possible.

"Good thing," Connor mumbled.

Turning the corner, he didn't see the well-dressed woman coming straight at him until it was almost too late. When he did, his hands shot out to keep from knocking her down.

Catching her breath, Megan felt her surprise immediately turn to pleasure as she realized she'd almost walked into her son. If she noticed the self-conscious way Connor dropped his hands to his side, she gave no indication.

"Connor, Lacy, I was just on my way up to see Ford to find out how everything went." She looked at Chase's sleeping face, and her heart melted.

The little boy looked so much like her other sons had. Like Connor must have at his age. She felt cheated and blessed at the same time. Cheated because she'd missed out on all those years, missed holding him to her heart instead of just keeping thoughts of him there. And blessed because fate had at least been kind enough to bring him back to her after all these years.

She refrained from caressing the sleeping child. Instead, she looked at Connor. "So, how did it go?"

"Fine." Connor bit off the word.

He was far from comfortable with this unexpected run-in. He was far from comfortable dealing with Megan at all, and it had nothing to do with the woman herself. The trouble was with him. Try as he might, Connor was still having trouble reconciling himself to the fact that the woman he had buried, the woman he had called mother for forty-five years of his life wasn't his mother. At first he thought time would help him come to terms with the situation, but in fact the opposite was true. He was finding it very difficult to accept Megan Maitland as his birth mother.

"The doctor said he has otitis media," Lacy offered when Connor gave no indication that he was going to elaborate for Megan. "We just picked up some medication for him." She nodded at the white bag in Connor's hand.

After all these years of association at the hospital, and with two doctors in the family, Megan was well acquainted with a variety of diagnoses. This, she knew, was a very common malady among children.

"Nothing to worry about," she assured, a soft, maternal smile curving her mouth. "Still, I can remember how afraid I was with Mitchell when he was a baby. I was sure he was going to die a thousand times over. I thought every sniffle was pneumonia, every fever the beginning of meningitis. And when he developed colic I thought the whole world was

going to come crashing to an end.'' Megan laughed
at the memory of the frightened first-time mother she
had been. ''But he managed to live through it all,
despite my inexperience. And so did I.'' She winked
at Lacy, sensing a kinship. ''You will, too. But if
you ever feel like you're at the end of your rope, just
call me. That's what I'm here for.'' Giving in to impulse, she hugged Lacy gently with one arm, careful
not to wake Chase. ''Thanks for calling me.'' She
meant that sincerely.

Lacy looked at her son, relieved that he continued
to doze, then raised her eyes to meet Megan's. If she
could have picked out her own mother, this would
have been the woman she would have chosen. Connor didn't know how lucky he was. ''It's nice to have
an in.''

Megan was aware that throughout the exchange,
Connor was standing to the side, impatiently silent.
Greedy for any tidbits she could get, Megan was reluctant to let him leave. She tried to get a few more
words out of him. Easy conversations, she knew,
were still not visible on the horizon, but she was
hoping to at least plant the seeds for a future crop.

''So, Connor, how is everything going otherwise?''

He knew she was only trying to be nice, but even
though it made no sense, even though he was angry
at Clarise for the deception his life had been envel-
oped in, there was still a feeling of disloyalty haunt-

ing him for acknowledging this woman as his mother. He felt unaccountably lost between two worlds, the one he'd known and had thought he'd belonged in, and the one he suddenly found himself in. Like a wounded dog that withdrew to a dark place in order to get well, he felt himself pulling back from the very people he knew he should be building bridges with. He couldn't explain it, not even to himself, but it was something he needed to try to work out.

"Fine," he replied.

Megan ignored the monosyllable, attempting to draw him out. "The ranch beginning to shape up? I hear—"

He stopped her before she could offer any sort of help, advice or the name of someone he could seek out. "It's shaping up just fine."

She knew this was hard for him, and because it was, she pushed her hurt feelings aside. With the patience that motherhood had brought her, Megan was determined to get through to him. "You know, as far as horse stock goes, I could talk to—"

What did it take for her to back off? He had to work this whole thing out for himself. "No need to talk to anyone for me. Things are progressing just fine."

He was angry and trying to bridle it. Megan knew when it was time to step back. Maybe next time things would go better.

"Well, then, I won't detain you any longer." She paused to kiss Chase's cheek. Still asleep, the baby fussed slightly. "I know, it's a pain being sick. But you'll be all right soon," she whispered to the child.

He should be feeling something, seeing his "mother" in a tender moment with his son, Connor thought. But all he felt was confusion. Confusion about Megan, about Chase and about Lacy. Perhaps most of all about Lacy. Damn. What he needed was the peace of a blank mind, at least for a while.

"We have to be going," Connor told Megan, his voice formal. "Thanks for getting the doctor to see him so fast."

The words stung, though she knew he hadn't meant them to. They were words that could have been offered to a stranger. "He's my grandson, Connor. There's no need to thank me."

That just made him feel even more awkward. "Yeah, well, thanks anyway." Connor tugged on the brim of his Stetson, signaling an end to the exchange.

Turning on the heel of his boot, he walked out quickly, assuming that Lacy and Chase were right behind him. He paused when he came to the hospital's entrance and looked over his shoulder. He swore silently. Lacy was still with Megan.

She gave Connor's mother an apologetic smile, knowing there was nothing she could say to soothe Megan. She squeezed the other woman's hand. "I'll work on him," she promised.

Before Megan could say anything, Lacy hurried after Connor.

The moment she was through the front door, Connor turned and strode through the lot, leading the way to his car.

He stayed a few steps ahead, wanting to avoid a confrontation. Instinct told him she was going to start picking apart his behavior at any moment.

When he unlocked the passenger side of the car, he could feel Lacy's eyes on him. It was just a matter of time, but he was hoping that she wouldn't say anything until they'd reached the house. Hoping that silence begat silence, he got into his vehicle and waited for her to strap herself in. When she did, he took his foot off the brake and backed out of the spot.

Well, it was obvious he wasn't going to say anything until she was, Lacy thought. Knowing Connor, he probably didn't even realize he'd trampled on Megan's heart with mud-encrusted boots.

"You were a little sharp with her, don't you think?"

Here it came. He could feel resentment beginning to take hold. He turned at the end of the block.

"That's none of your business."

Lacy had expected nothing less, but it still hurt when she heard the rebuff. "Well, she's Chase's grandmother, and what affects him affects me, so…yes, I'd say it was my business."

He spared her an annoyed glance, but she pushed

on, surprising herself with her nerve. The old Lacy would have closed her mouth and retreated. The old Lacy wouldn't have even ventured this far. But the old Lacy had felt she had something to lose. This Lacy didn't.

"You know, Connor, I know this isn't easy for you, suddenly being surrounded by people who care about you, what you're into, your plans, your dreams, how you're doing, how you're feeling." Sarcasm thickened her voice. "Must really be rough, but for the sake of chivalry, I think maybe, just maybe, you could be a shade politer to these people. They don't know they're interfering with your life."

For a second, he was speechless. No matter how prepared he thought he was for her, Lacy just kept on shocking him. "What the hell crawled into your bonnet and bit you?"

"Nothing." She raised her chin. "Except maybe never having any of that. Ever." The world really wasn't fair, was it? She would have given anything to have what he had. And he was turning his back on it because it didn't suit him. The jerk. "Makes me kind of think it's wasted on you."

He kept his eyes on the road. They were coming to the outskirts of the city. When he spoke, his voice was hard. "Maybe it is."

They drove in silence for a little while. He'd always liked silence; it was something he could get lost in. This time it felt like some sort of oppressive burden he was struggling to get out from under.

Finally, he couldn't take it anymore. Though it was unspoken, he could feel her disapproval. Why that should matter, he didn't explore. Its existence irritated him. "So what is it you want me to do?"

Startled, she looked at him. He hadn't said a single word for at least twenty minutes. "About what?"

Damn it, why was she playing coy? He realized he was gripping the wheel and loosened his hold slightly. "About...*them*."

Lacy sighed. Maybe this was all useless, but she had to try. For Chase's sake as well as the big, dumb lug she was sitting next to.

"I don't want you to *do* anything. I just thought maybe you could be nicer to them. Accept their help when they offer it. You were almost surly when Jake came to install those fixtures in the ceiling for you."

Annoyance almost got the better of him. He might have known she'd bring that up. "I didn't ask him to."

Was he really that thickheaded, or was it his heart that suffered from a condition? "No, you didn't. That's the whole point. He did it just the same, even though you didn't ask." When he didn't say anything, she added, "It's called caring."

Connor snorted at the idea. If he didn't know any better, he would have said Lacy still believed in fairy tales. At the very least, her approach to life was hopelessly simpleminded. "How the hell can he really care about me? Jake Maitland never even laid eyes on me until a few months ago."

This was something time didn't enter into. "I knew I loved Chase the minute I saw him."

The woman was comparing apples to oranges. Typical. That's what happened when you led with your heart instead of your head. Your thinking got muddled. "That's different. He's your son."

He was missing the point again, she thought. "He's my blood, and in the end, blood will tell. You and Jake are connected in the most basic of ways. Megan's blood flows through both of you."

He'd wound up apologizing to Jake that day. The odd thing about it was that Jake seemed to understand the turmoil that had him pushing away his newfound family. Connor supposed he was behaving like an ass. His annoyance gave way to amusement. Glancing at her, he shook his head. "You know, I don't remember you being able to argue the ears off a brass monkey before."

She caught the glint of a smile on his face, and it felt as if a ray of sunshine had burst inside her. "And I never thought of you as a brass monkey before," she replied with a grin. "Truce?"

There was something engaging about her when she grinned like that. Hell, if he were being honest with himself—something that seemed pretty damn dangerous to do right about now—he'd have to say there was something engaging about her no matter what she was doing. He tried to keep his mind on the road and the conversation, not on the woman beside him, who seemed to arouse him with every breath she took and every rise and fall of her firm, small breasts.

Connor pretended to clear his throat when it was actually his thoughts he was clearing. "I wasn't aware that we had gone to war."

"Not war, exactly," she said, "but there were definitely the makings of a major skirmish about the conversation we were just having." She settled back, contenting herself with looking at his profile. It was the kind that made a woman feel safe. Rugged, powerful, with just the slightest touch that gave the heart hope there was some sensitivity existing beneath. "I really don't want to argue with you."

"Could have fooled me." But for once, he was smiling as he said it.

"It's just that I would have given my eyeteeth to have people like that in my life," Lacy went on. "All I had was an aunt, and she didn't live nearly as long as I would have wanted her to."

She had been left alone. Alone to cope with a world that was too often cold, too often distant.

He supposed he could see things from her perspective. Women needed family, friends, a loving network of support. Men didn't. Or at least he didn't. He'd been raised differently, taught to keep his distance from everyone and everything. Which made having Lacy in his life hard.

"Well, you're welcome to the Maitlands if you want them. Me, I just like being by myself."

For a moment, she tried to picture embracing that way of life—and failed.

"You know, I can't imagine that. Oh, I can see being comfortable with yourself, enjoying your own company and all that. That's a good thing. But not to want a family—" Lacy shook her head, unable to fathom such a thing. "Not to want to know that there were people who would go out of their way for you just because you were part of them—I'm afraid that just doesn't compute for me."

He didn't think that made him so odd. Independent was more like it. It was a good thing for a man to stand up on his own. Dependence bred weakness, made a man soft. And ripe for disappointment. Like a man who'd just discovered the life he'd known had been a lie.

"It's a matter of what you're used to," he told her bluntly. "If you've never had it, you don't miss it."

That was where he was very wrong. "Not always. Trust me."

He paused, wondering about her. If he asked her about her past, would she interpret it as something other than idle curiosity? Probably. She was forever misinterpreting things one way or another no matter what he said or didn't say. This would be no different. The best thing was to walk away from it and leave it alone.

It surprised him to hear himself asking, "What was it like? Your childhood." He tacked the last two words on when he realized he wasn't being clear.

That was easy. Lacy could sum it up in one word. "Lonely." A rueful expression crossed her face. "My aunt was a great person, but I just wanted more. A regular family. The American dream, I guess."

The wistful longing in her voice bothered him. And that bothered him, as well. He didn't want to have feelings about her. He wanted to give her no more thought than he did the horse auctioneer he'd seen the other day or the pharmacist who'd given him Chase's medicine.

Too late. Striving for at least the appearance of indifference, Connor lifted one shoulder in a half shrug. "Maybe you'll have it one day."

He said it with no promise, no hint of anything that was to come. It wasn't himself he was including in that mix, Lacy thought. The words "one day" were vague throwaways. They had nothing to do with him or any feelings he might have for her.

Because he didn't have any, Lacy reminded herself. How many times did she have to be hit over the head with that before it finally sank in?

She banked down her feelings, pushed them away. It wasn't herself she was supposed to be thinking of, but Chase. And Connor. "You know, it might be nice if you invited her over."

That came completely out of the blue. He turned to look at her. "Who?"

"Your mother."

What the hell was she saying? "My mother's dead—" And then it came back to him all over again. "Oh, yeah, right."

She saw confusion and then resignation crease his brow. Her heart went out to him. "Takes some getting used to, doesn't it?"

"Yeah, it does." His voice was a tad curt. "And I don't think so."

Was he talking about her idea to invite Megan over to the ranch, or something else? "How's that again?"

"I don't think she'd want to come over to see the place. Megan," he clarified.

"You never know until you ask, and I happen to think she might." Lacy ventured out on a limb, even though she knew Connor probably resented her butting in. "Every mother wants to see where her son lives."

He liked things to be straightforward, without any need for second guessing. "Then why didn't she ask to see it?"

He did have a lot to learn, Lacy mused. "Because she's waiting to be asked. She's not the type to just barge in without an invitation."

Connor spared her a glance. "There's a lot to be said for that."

She knew that he was referring to the way she was behaving. Well, too bad. She'd done the demure act when that was what she'd felt, but looking back, it certainly hadn't gotten her an inch closer to where she wanted to be. The only way things happened, she thought, was if you went out and did them. If you grabbed life with both hands. She wasn't the two-fisted type, but she was learning. One fist at a time.

Ignoring his not-so-veiled hint, she doggedly pushed forward. "So are you going to invite her over?"

"Maybe." He didn't have to look at Lacy to see that wasn't good enough. He knew she was about to launch into another verbal assault. He wasn't up to it. "Yeah, okay. I'll invite her."

"When?"

He might have known it wouldn't end here. "When I get good and ready," he snapped.

Oh, no, she wasn't about to back off now, not when she'd gotten him all this way. "And when will that be?"

He swore under his breath. "You don't give up, do you?"

This was the new, improved Lacy, and she was determined not to regress. "Giving up is for quitters, and I've decided I'm not going to be a quitter anymore."

She sounded so serious. "When were you ever a quitter?"

Except for that one night together, he'd probably never even noticed her enough to realize how shy and retiring she'd been. "Not taking part in the game is as good as being a quitter."

Their eyes met in the rearview mirror. "Any particular game you're referring to?"

"Life." She knew what he was trying to do. "You didn't answer the question, you know. About when you're going to ask your mother over."

Junkyard dogs had nothing on Lacy. He gave in. "One day's as good as another. You pick."

"Okay."

He knew she meant it. And that he had voluntarily sealed his own doom. He couldn't help but wonder just what the hell had come over him lately. Was a time he wouldn't have been nearly this damn soft.

In the back seat, they could hear Chase stirring. Lacy twisted in her seat to look at their son. She saw his lashes fluttering, although he hadn't opened his eyes yet.

"Uh-oh, I think the shot's beginning to wear off." The ranch house could just be seen in the distance. "Good thing we're almost home."

"Yeah."

It had an odd, comforting sound to it, he thought. Home. He tried not to let his mind wander to the ramifications of the word. She'd turned down his proposal. The home they were making was for Chase. For now, he left it at that.

CHAPTER NINE

SHE WAS RIGHT. Chase was better.

But then, Connor thought, tiptoeing out of the newly renovated nursery, leaving Chase sound asleep behind him, Lacy knew more than he did. He was willing to admit that. When it came to kids, she knew a hell of a lot more than he did.

Not that that was hard, Connor thought, amused. He knew next to nothing. Very softly, he pulled the door shut behind him. He found himself completely lost in this maze called fatherhood. He secretly counted himself lucky that Lacy was there to pick up the slack, of which there was a great deal. Watching her, he had to admit she was a natural at this baby thing. As he looked back over the last few weeks, he realized that he was getting used to her confidence, but it did still surprise him at times. He'd remembered what she'd been like back when she'd first worked with him. Not sure her shadow was her own.

Now she had enough confidence to order him around. Like this morning. She'd handed Chase to him and asked that he put the little boy down for a nap. He'd protested that the baby didn't look sleepy and she'd said, nice as you please, that he'd fall asleep. He'd walked off with Chase in his arms, feeling awkward, feeling something warm stir inside him. Especially when the little boy had looked at him and smiled.

And damned if Chase didn't fall asleep. She'd been right about that and right about the fever thing. Yesterday, when they'd taken him to see the doctor, Chase had been burning up. Today, he was practically cool as the flank of a horse standing in a corral in January. Just warm enough to let you know that everything was all right.

Of course, being right about the baby didn't mean she was right about everything else, he thought, making his way down the stairs. And he was going to tell her so, just as soon as he found her.

The thing she was least right about was trying to push him together with his family. She'd been up to that the minute she'd found out he *had* a family. Pushing first from one angle, then another, trying all sides until she found one that gave.

Connor frowned as he came to the landing. He'd hired Lacy—at her insistence—to be his cook. That meant she was supposed to cook, not meddle.

He knew he was going to have to set her straight about that. Given her personality change, she wouldn't stop unless she was made to stop. The sooner he talked to her about this, the better—before she did anything else he was going to regret.

She wasn't in the library, where he'd left her, the library being the latest room she'd placed under siege. Her renovations were galloping along. If they had a poll to name the next hurricane that came through Texas, he was going to see about putting Lacy on the list, he thought, walking into the hall.

"Lacy. Lacy!" he called, raising his voice when she didn't answer.

"In here."

Here turned out to be the kitchen. When he entered, he found her on a ladder, stretching even though she was perched on the top rung. It didn't aid his intended crusade against her, but he couldn't help pausing to watch as she reached up, her young body taut, her breasts straining against the confines of a tucked-in white cotton blouse that didn't seem to want to give her enough room to move.

There was no getting away from it. Motherhood had ripened her body, perfecting what had once been merely near perfect.

He realized that his mouth had gone dry while other parts of him had become just the slightest bit enlivened. Damn, he was going to have to work at exercising more control over his thoughts.

"Don't you know better than to climb up that high?" he snapped, more annoyed with himself and his reaction than the recklessness of what she was doing.

What *was* she doing, anyway? She looked as if

she was rummaging for something on top of the pantry—except there was nothing there.

"What?" Not hearing him, Lacy turned her head
and, without thinking, partially turned her body, as
well. It was enough to throw her slightly off kilter—
and the ladder off balance.

To Connor's horror, the ladder began to lean.

Lacy tried to compensate, but it was too late. Connor got to her just in time to catch her as the ladder
went crashing down.

Air flew out of Lacy's lungs as she landed in his
arms with a jolt she could feel clear up to her scalp.
It took her a second to find her voice. When she did,
she found a smile that went along with it and aimed
it straight for his heart.

"Nice catch."

A flurry of oaths flew through Connor's mind. At
the last moment, he managed to keep them back.
"Why didn't you scream?" Most women would
have screamed. Hell, most men would have yelled,
he thought. Yet she'd flown, silent, like an angel who
suddenly found herself plunging to earth.

Shock had stolen her tongue, but Lacy figured it
was more mysterious to smile at him, now that the
accident had ended well—except for maybe the ladder, she corrected, glancing at it. She'd have to check
it out before she climbed up again.

There was complete trust in her eyes. "I knew you
were going to catch me."

The ache Connor was feeling through his body had absolutely nothing to do with the weight in his arms. He'd handled feed bags that were heavier.

Damn, but he wanted her.

Belatedly, Connor realized she'd wrapped her arms around his neck and he liked it. It brought her body closer against his, igniting a warmth he found, much to his distress, that he needed. "Oh, you did, did you?"

She nodded, her eyes never leaving his. "You're kind of like an unsung hero. Don't talk much, don't even seem to be paying attention, but when someone needs you, you're right there." Like he'd been with his offer to care for his son—and her, she thought. "You wouldn't have let me fall."

He raised a brow, attempting to seem blasé. Attempting not to look affected by her closeness. "I was going for the ladder."

Lacy glanced at it. It had landed against the table, its topmost rungs forming a forty-five-degree angle against the table's surface.

A grin played along her lips. "Well, then I guess you missed. But I don't think the ladder's going to mind. It doesn't look broken."

Which brought him back to anger. Didn't she have any sense in her head? "But you could have been. What the hell were you doing up there?"

"Dusting."

Was she out of her mind? "Who the hell is going

to see dust up there? Who's even going to. *know* there's dust up there?''

''Me.'' She knew it was probably silly, but she'd begun tidying, and one thing had just led to another. Just like coming into Connor's home to work for him had led her to love him. ''I want everything to be perfect tonight.''

''Having you in a body cast wouldn't be so perfect.'' And then he backed up as her words sank in. An uneasy suspicion began to filter through him. ''What's tonight?''

Lacy held her breath. ''Your mother's coming over for dinner, remember?''

The moment was gone.

With a surge of annoyance, Connor put her down, ignoring the electrical impulses that went off through his body as hers brushed against it.

He scowled at her. ''No, I don't remember.'' What the hell was she doing, taking it upon herself to throw his doors open like this?

''Yes, you do,'' she insisted quietly. Firmly. ''Yesterday, in the car, you said I could pick a day, and when we got home I said how about tomorrow night for dinner. You said yes. Muttered it, actually.'' Mentally crossing her fingers, she watched his expression.

A vague recollection of the exchange of words came to him, though what their content was, he couldn't have said even under oath.

Restless, he began to pace, eyeing Lacy all the while. Trying to keep his anger under control. "So you invited my mother to dinner?"

Her eyes never left him. This was what Daniel Boone must have felt like, facing down the bear in the old legend. "I thought it was a good start."

He wasn't going to be forced into anything. Lacy was going to have to call the woman and cancel, that was all there was to it. He glared in her direction. "Think again."

Inside, she felt her stomach quiver, but she held her ground. This was important. For him and the baby. And for Megan. "Don't you think forty-five years is enough time to go by without getting to know her?"

Where the hell did she get off, doing this to him? "Like you said, forty-five years have gone by. A few more days won't matter."

It was an excuse, and he knew it. She had to get him to admit that. "They will if they knit themselves into weeks and then years."

He lifted a shoulder indifferently, then let it fall, not answering. He headed for the doorway. Why hadn't he gone with his first instincts and left for the corral after he'd put Chase down? Having sought her out to tell her the baby was asleep had been a mistake he meant to rectify now.

"Cancel it," he ordered.

Hurrying, Lacy swerved around him and reached

the doorway before Connor did. She placed her small body in his way. "I've never thought of you as being a coward before."

Her words rankled him, and anger smoldered within him, threatening to spill out. "What are you talking about? I'm not a coward."

There were many definitions of the word. Her eyes were soft as she looked at him. "Then what do you call avoiding seeing your mother?"

He didn't care for pity, didn't give it and certainly didn't accept it. He resented that she felt she had to offer it. "Enjoying my privacy—which has gone all to hell since you moved in."

He knew exactly how to hit her where it would hurt the most. Lacy raised her chin, but he saw the pain that had sprung up in her eyes. She couldn't fool him.

"I can move out." With that, she turned on her heel to walk out.

Connor caught a sucker punch right to the gut as guilt slammed into him with the force of a runaway freight train. He grabbed her hand before she could make good her exit. Though they'd been born of frustration, he'd regretted the words the second he'd spoken them.

"Lacy, I'm sorry."

Debating whether or not to pull her hand out of his grasp and continue walking, Lacy blew out a breath, then turned to look at him. It served no purpose to hold on to her hurt and anger. Nothing productive would come of it. Besides, she didn't like feeling this way, as if there was a grudge between them.

"Apology accepted." A smile began to take root, working its way slowly over raw terrain. "So you promise you won't duck out on me tonight?" She knew he was more than capable of it.

He sighed. She was one step ahead of him. "I promise I won't duck out on you tonight. Why do you care so much about her?"

He still had trouble calling Megan his mother, didn't know if he could ever really manage it and not feel as if he was choking on the words. In his mind, the term had become synonymous with deception.

She placed her hand on his shoulder, silently comforting the agitation she knew existed beneath his steely exterior.

"Because I understand what she must have gone through, losing a baby. And what she must be going through to have discovered that her lost baby is now a strapping forty-five-year-old man who was kept from her all these years." Her eyes eloquently pleaded for him to open up his heart at least this much. It didn't matter that Megan had seven other children or that Connor was an adult, not a child. They needed each other. "She wants to make up for some of that lost time.

"But most of all, I care about you—how this affects you," Lacy added, knowing she'd let too much out. She didn't want him backing away, afraid that she might have ideas about the two of them. She didn't. Any ideas that might exist were buried in her pillow, along with her tears. "You're Chase's father, and he's going to take a lot of his cues from you."

Connor frowned. He hardly thought of himself as a role model. "He'd be better off not doing that."

Did he think he had to be a plaster saint for his son to look up to him? Lacy wondered. His flaws were what made him human. And lovable. She hadn't fallen in love with a cast-iron hero. She loved a man. But Lacy knew that argument wouldn't work. So, resignedly, she murmured, "Your opinion. Not mine."

He saw it. Saw the flash of love in her eyes. Saw the look that had undone him in the first place, cutting through his haze of alcohol and self-pity that night his mother had died. He still was lucid enough then to have wanted her. Her softness, her strength. Her love.

It all came barreling back. "Damn it, Lacy, if you had an ounce of sense in you..."

Something warm cloaked itself over her shoulders, drawing her to him. She raised her eyes to his, and her heart began to hammer erratically. "I'd what? If I had an ounce of sense in me, I'd what?"

He was going to say *flee,* but he never managed to get around to forming the single word.

Instead, in one swift movement, Connor pulled her into his arms and sealed his mouth to hers. The way he'd wanted to all this time. All these days and long, endless nights when he'd lain in bed, aware that she was close by. Just out of reach.

Always out of reach.

If he'd had any strength of character, he would have let her continue to be out of reach. But he didn't, not when it came to Lacy.

What he had was a deep-seated hunger for all the things she was, all the things she brought to him so selflessly.

Electricity zipped through Lacy's veins the instant his lips came down on hers. It had nothing to do with the dry, cracking air and everything to do with the man who knew how to make her heart sing without ever having heard the melody himself.

She knew he didn't love her, that kissing her until she was practically mindless was just feeding some physical need he was trying to tame, but she didn't care. Because kissing him fed something so much greater for her.

She needed this.

Despite her newfound bravado and the backbone she had managed to grow so late in her young life, Lacy needed the feel of Connor's strong arms around her, the press of his hard body against her. The taste of his lips as they sapped every ounce of energy out of her.

Her mind spun, drunk with the moment, with the man. Savoring both because she knew how rare this moment was.

How was it that each time he kissed her, he only wanted more? That rather than becoming immune, he found himself more addicted to her and all the things she seemed to be? He felt like someone with no willpower, giving in to a decadent pleasure he'd sworn off. A pleasure that would do harm not only to him, but to her.

He tried to focus on that, on what he owed the mother of his son.

With almost superhuman effort, Connor drew back, taking the arms that had wrapped themselves around his neck and disentangling them. He allowed himself a moment to look into her eyes as he held her hands in his.

"All right, Lacy, you've won. Have the dinner."

Her heart was slamming against her rib cage so hard, she wasn't sure if she would ever draw breath rhythmically again. How could she be so affected when he was just the opposite—cool and removed?

Because only one of them was in love here, she reminded herself. And it wasn't him.

She'd known that before the kiss and would know that long after this moment was history. Squaring her shoulders, she made the best of it. The reluctant host had just surrendered.

"With you?" she prodded, cocking her head as she eyed him.

Why did he want to kiss her again? He'd just satisfied that impulse, so why was it hounding him again as if he were a man fresh off a fast, dying for that first morsel of food?

Because he hadn't satisfied the impulse, he'd only tantalized it, he told himself. He knew his only salvation was to concentrate on the dinner and not the woman.

"Yes, with me. What time is this all happening?" Not that timing mattered, he thought. He had nothing to escape to this evening.

Time was something she hadn't specified yet. "Your mother said she could be here any time after six. Since we usually have dinner at seven, I thought—" Lacy held her breath, waiting for him to make an excuse.

"Seven'll be fine."

His easy acceptance was unexpected, and she smiled at him, hoping to erase that stoic expression from his face. He looked as if he had just agreed to the time of his execution and was determined to meet it without showing any emotion whatsoever.

"It'll be all right, Connor," she assured him softly.

"Yeah. Whatever." He shrugged. Afraid he might

take her into his arms again, he shoved his hands into his back pockets. "I came to tell you I'm going to be down at the stables for a while. They're bringing in the new mares I bought at auction last week."

She thought that after he woke up from his nap, she might take Chase to the corral with her. "Need any company?"

"No." He began to walk out of the room, then stopped and retraced his steps to the ladder. He folded the two sides together and then picked it up. Holding it in exactly the center, he managed to balance the ends as he began to carry it out.

She watched his progress, following from behind. "What are you doing?"

"Making sure you don't get the urge to become airborne again." That was all he said as he left.

She knew she should have been annoyed, but all she could do was smile.

CHAPTER TEN

"THIS IS WONDERFUL, Lacy. I knew you were a good cook from my meals at the diner, but you've surpassed yourself tonight." It wasn't her habit to eat much, but the roast pork loin had been so good, Megan found she couldn't resist a second serving.

Wiping off the applesauce that Chase insisted on wearing instead of eating, Lacy savored the compliment. Praise was something she never took for granted. "Well, you're welcome to come here anytime you like for the meal of your choice—breakfast, lunch or dinner."

Though she wasn't looking in his direction, Lacy could feel Connor's eyes on her, heated by the invitation she had extended to his mother without bothering to consult him. She had a feeling that one way or another, whether he railed or gave her the silent treatment, she was going to pay for trespassing into his territory. But there hadn't been any way to throw the ball into his court without an awkward pause.

She glanced at him and saw that he didn't exactly look pleased.

Too bad. You've got a family, get used to it. And be damn grateful that you're one of the lucky ones.

"Maybe I will, at that." Megan's eyes shifted to her son. She hesitated slightly. "Provided I wouldn't be intruding."

She knew, he thought. Megan Maitland knew how hard this was for him. How difficult it was turning out to be to put his house, so to speak, in order and get accustomed to a completely new set of tenants.

"No," he finally said, albeit slowly, "you wouldn't be intruding."

It would take more than lip service to convince her. Megan didn't want to be treated like a guest, she wanted to find a way to become part of all this.

"So." She set down her napkin, looking at Lacy, who was wiping Chase's sticky fingers. "What can I do to help? Dishes? Entertain this fine young man?" She made no effort to hide her eagerness to pitch in.

"I can entertain myself," Connor replied quietly.

Exchanging glances with Lacy, Megan failed to keep the corners of her mouth from rising in amusement. "I was talking about Chase."

Connor muttered something unintelligible and looked away. Megan's smile deepened.

"The dishwasher can do the dishes," Lacy assured her, rising. She gathered the three dinner plates, piling one on the other and placing the flatware on top. "I'll just slip them into the machine."

Megan started to reach for the glasses. "Well, let me help you clear them—"

But Lacy was already pushing her hands away. "No, that's all right, really. You're a guest." Picking up the plates, she headed for the kitchen. "Why don't you and Connor get further acquainted while I just pop these into the dishwater?"

There she went, orchestrating things again, Connor thought. Doing things she had no business doing. "We already are acquainted," he informed her.

"That's why I used the word further," Lacy responded cheerfully over her shoulder. She looked pointedly at Connor. "Talk about Chase—that should get you started. Or even better, your horses." Of course, Lacy realized. He loved horses. That was a subject he enjoyed talking about. "The herd is coming along quite nicely," she confided to Megan, then disappeared into the kitchen, dishes in hand.

Megan found herself wishing she had a coffee cup to toy with. But dessert was yet to come. She shifted her eyes to her son. He looked like a soft-footed creature trying to find a comfortable way to stand on a beach covered with burning sand.

"She really is something else, isn't she?" Megan said fondly.

"Yeah." The answer was both dark and grudgingly surrendered.

Megan shook her head. She could almost read his

thoughts. "I have a feeling you don't mean that phrase in quite the same way I do."

She had that right, he thought. He eyed the whiskey decanter on the hutch and wondered if it would be considered bad form to have some before dessert. He knew he could do with a shot to help him endure the evening. "You don't live with her."

"No, I'm not lucky enough for that." He looked incredulous at her choice of words. "But she reminds me a great deal of Abby at that age." Leaning forward, Megan folded her hands on the table. "I say we follow her suggestion. Tell me about the herd."

He noticed she didn't take up Lacy's first suggestion, to talk about Chase. He wondered if that was by design or by chance, since he knew the little boy was of far more interest to her than horses. "It's growing."

The strong, silent type, that was what her firstborn had turned out to be. Megan harvested each word. "Are you planning on raising breeding stock or—"

"Racehorses."

The answer surprised her. She thought of racing in terms of taking chances. He looked like the type who liked a sure thing. "I see. Have you been interested in racing long?"

The shrug was indifferent, and his look went right through her, as if she was part of the embroidered upholstery on the back of the chair. "A while."

She'd always been intuitive. Megan could sense

what he was going through. And she ached for him. She placed her hand on his shoulder, thinking how broad and strong it was.

"Connor, I know this is probably harder for you than it is for me." She saw a question enter his eyes and elaborated. "For me, there's only joy. And I want you to know that I'm willing to wait however long it takes for you to become comfortable with this situation."

Unable to sit any longer, he rose to his feet, towering over her. "How can there be only joy? People deceived you. Your own father took away something that rightfully belonged to you, deprived you of your own flesh and blood—"

She'd already made her peace with that. "He thought he was doing it for the right reasons."

He didn't understand. "But he still did it. And you were still lied to."

Because he was on his feet, she rose, too. "Yes, but it won't do my heart any good to dwell on that. There's nothing to be gained from this kind of anger, Connor. And I have you in my life now." She wished she could hug him. Could hold him for a moment, bonding with him. But she knew he wasn't a toucher. Clarise wouldn't have raised him to be. "I might not have any memories of your first steps or any of the wonderful moments that mark a child's passage from one stage to another, but you're here now, and I'm grateful for that. Grateful for the chance to attempt to bridge the gap between us.'' She didn't want to cloud whatever time they had together with recriminations about the past.

He stood looking at her for a long moment, amazed at the sincerity of her words. ''You really mean that, don't you?''

She nodded slowly. ''With all my heart.''

He felt his mouth curving. ''It really is a hell of a heart, you know that?''

She could feel them forming. Tears. She didn't want to cry now. Men never understood tears, especially when those men were your own children. ''All I know is that it never felt quite as full as it does now.''

It was her tone more than the look on her face that got to him. He felt something from years back rising in his chest. ''You make it hard to hold back.''

''I was hoping for that.''

Giving in, he took her into his arms and hugged her. Hugged the woman who had given him life.

Megan pressed her lips together, holding back tears she knew would only make him uncomfortable again.

''Connor—'' her voice was hoarse ''—do you think you could find it in your own heart to someday call me Mother?'' She felt him drawing back. She didn't want this moment to end. She'd waited so long to hug her son, to hold him in her arms just once. When she'd asked her father, after the delivery, if she could hold the child he'd told her was stillborn, to say goodbye, he'd said he didn't think it was a good idea, and she had meekly gone along, even though her heart had screamed, *"No."* Now she knew why.

"I don't mean now," she told Connor quickly, not wanting to lose him again. "I know that would be asking too much, but maybe someday, if—"

Connor saw the tears in her eyes. He was doing battle with some moisture of his own, surprised that he could be so moved after all these years. Except for the day of Clarise's funeral, he hadn't felt the need to shed tears since he'd been a boy.

He felt something threaten to choke off the air in his throat. "Mother," he said quietly, looking at her.

"Oh, I do like the sound of that." Unable to hold back, Megan put her arms around her firstborn again, and this time sobbed her happiness against his broad chest.

Connor didn't mind. He closed his arms around his mother.

Standing in the doorway where she was confident neither one saw her, Lacy smiled.

Mission accomplished, she congratulated herself.

Very quietly, she slipped into the kitchen. They were going to want dessert eventually.

"Pretty proud of yourself, aren't you?"

Lacy turned from the door they had just closed on

Megan. Connor's mother had remained for another two hours, going on a tour of the house and then helping Lacy put Chase to bed. Lacy had been secretly thrilled to share the activity with Megan. It made her feel as if she were part of the family, as well, instead of on the outside, wistfully looking in.

Delighted with bringing Connor and his mother closer together, she looked at him with feigned innocence. "Why, Connor, whatever do you mean?"

"You know damn well what I mean." But he couldn't bring himself to be annoyed, though he knew that might be the safer way to go. He had the uneasy feeling she had become one of those people who, if you gave them an inch, suddenly built a condo on it, complete with an iron-clad lease.

He was glad she'd done this, she thought in satisfaction, searching his face. "Do I?"

He snorted. "That smug look on your face says it all."

Her smile widened. She couldn't have felt better right now even if someone had handed her a check for a million dollars. "Then there's no need to ask, is there?"

He had to stop thinking how adorable she looked. "This doesn't give you the right to meddle in other things, you know."

She doubted that he was talking about them. "There aren't any other things to meddle in."

"Right." He'd almost said too much, he thought.

That came from having her linger on his mind. "But just in case you get something in your head—"

Was he talking about them? "Yes?"

When she looked at him like that, he found his mouth growing dry. "Don't," he concluded. "Just don't."

High on success, she let herself float a little longer, pretending that she'd guessed right. That what was circling his mind was the way things stood between the two of them. Maybe, just maybe, bringing him together with his mother had, however temporarily, aroused other emotions. Emotions involving her.

Her eyes played along his face, memorizing every plane, loving every inch. "That's rather a broad command, don't you think?"

Damn, but she was getting to him. She was doing nothing except standing here talking to him, yet she was getting to him as surely as if she'd just been injected into his arm directly, like life-giving serum. He struggled to sound distant. "It was meant to be."

She didn't expect any thanks, but she wanted something, a small positive acknowledgment, just this once. "Tell me you don't feel better for this."

His eyes locked with hers. "I don't feel better for this."

Any six-year-old could have seen he didn't mean it. It was written all over his face. "Liar." Lacy laughed at him. "When you finally leaped over that chasm you created yourself, you lit up like a jack-o'-lantern at Halloween.''

''A jack-o'-lantern?'' Connor echoed incredulously. ''You're comparing me to a damn gutted pumpkin? The least you could do, after what you've done, is say I lit up like a star-filled sky or a Christmas tree, not some overgrown squash with a gland condition.''

She went into the kitchen and began straightening up. Taking the dishes out of the dishwasher and putting them away. ''Didn't do much trick-or-treating, I take it.''

Other than dressing up as a Native American one year for a Halloween pageant when he was eight, he'd never donned a costume. ''No.''

She'd only been kidding. The negative answer gave them something else in common. ''Neither did I.''

''Neighbors too far apart?'' That had been the excuse Clarise had given him. It had been too much trouble to take him around.

She shook her head. ''No costume and—'' She shrugged away the rest. ''Never mind.'' With a shove, she pushed the pot she'd used to make the roast into the bottom cupboard.

This wasn't like her. So far, she'd seemed to make a point to share everything, to tell him far more than he wanted to know. ''No, come on, what?''

She turned away, taking the flatware out of the

machine. Wiping each piece one after the other, she returned them to the drawer. Her back remained to him. "I don't want to talk about it."

Curious, Connor leaned a hip on the counter, eyeing her. "Oh, you can gut me like a fish, inspecting all my insides inch by inch, but when it comes to your secrets, then it's never mind? Uh-uh, the game's not played that way. Spill it."

He wasn't going to go away until she gave him an answer, she realized.

"Nothing to spill. Most of my childhood wasn't exactly the kind they write fairy tales or sitcoms about. By the time I went to live with my aunt, she thought I was too old for 'such foolishness.'" Because she'd dearly loved the woman, Lacy had reconciled herself to the fact that Halloween, with its laughter, candy and costumes, was for others to enjoy, not her.

Foolishness. It didn't sound like something she'd say, he thought. Connor guessed that was her aunt's word, not hers. "How old were you?"

"Ten."

At ten, he could picture her with pigtails, a wall-to-wall grin and eyes that rivaled Fourth of July sparklers. "Ten hardly seems old, unless you're a house pet."

Connor paused, knowing this was the perfect opportunity to walk away from her. Lacy was feeling vulnerable and for once was protecting her territory instead of invading his. But, perfect or not, he found he couldn't get himself to do it—precisely because she was so vulnerable. He felt very protective, even though deep down he knew he should probably get his head examined.

"So, what else were you not allowed to do besides trick-or-treating?"

Finished unloading, she closed the dishwasher door. "I didn't mean to make it sound that way. I wasn't deprived, I just—hey." Light dawning, she swung around abruptly to face him.. "Wait a minute, we were discussing you, not me."

Catching her against the wall, he leaned his hand against it just above her head. All this banter had him feeling like some kid in high school. "I'd rather do you."

She knew he didn't mean it the way it sounded, but she couldn't resist teasing. "Really?"

Something serious slipped into his eyes and his expression. "Really."

Excitement rippled through her. She banked it down, knowing that she was fooling herself. There was nothing going on between them.

"That's twice you've lied in the last ten minutes," she accused him. "One more time, and your nose is going to start to grow." She ran the tip of her finger over the bridge of his nose. Even such a little action warmed her. She was hopeless, she told herself.

"You're just trying to make me forget that I just had a major victory here."

He didn't even bother to contest her words. Something felt as if it had opened up inside him tonight, and he knew he owed it all to her and her stubborn pigheadedness. But he wasn't about to tell her so. She would become unbearable to live with.

"Don't let it go to your head."

Lacy heard what she wanted to hear. "So, you admit it."

"I admit nothing." He couldn't quite carry off his neutral expression. She made him feel like singing. Like standing out in the rain and tilting his head back like some damned stupid turkey.

"C'mon, admit it." She laughed, doubling her fists and pretending to beat on his side—as if she could make a dent. "Admit that I did a good thing getting you and your mother together and talking. Admit that you wanted this."

"You're getting carried away."

"That's because I'm right."

"Okay, you're right. And for such a little thing, you've also got a hell of a right fist." He caught both fists in his hands, holding them still. "How long do you intend on pounding me?"

She looked at her immobilized hands. "I guess I'm about done now."

He opened his hands, releasing her. "I see this really is a red-letter day."

She was surprised to hear him admit it. He'd made even more progress than she'd thought. "Why, because you and your mother finally connected?"

"No," he said, deadpan, "because you backed off and gave up."

She pretended to sniff. "The day I do it over something important, that'll be your red-letter day, not before then."

The woman struck him as a tireless crusader. And one royal pain in his butt. "You like bashing your head against a wall?"

He made her sound far more obstinate than she saw herself. "Only when the wall finally caves in."

"And if it doesn't?"

He was talking about them, she thought. About him. "I make sure I have a giant supply of aspirin on hand."

In an incredibly magnanimous mood, he laughed, shaking his head. "She was right."

"Who?"

"My mother." He realized, pleased, that he hadn't hesitated this time when uttering the precious word. Mother. Megan Maitland was his mother. Maybe it was time he acted as if he was damn grateful to Lacy for what she'd done. "She said you were something else."

"I bet you were quick to jump in and tell her just what that something was—or were the words that came to your mind a bit too spicy for mixed company?''

''The only thing in this house that's spicy is you,'' he told her.

Maybe it was the evening, or the breakthrough he'd just experienced. Whatever it was, there was an exhilarating feeling racing through him, infusing every part of his being until he was certain he really could have lit up the sky.

His eyes on hers, he combed his fingers through Lacy's hair, framing her face. Bringing it closer to him.

''And I've suddenly got this overwhelming craving for spicy.''

''By all means,'' she murmured against his lips, excitement filtering through every pore, ''indulge your craving.''

CHAPTER ELEVEN

TINGLING sensations ran along her body, growing stronger as his kiss deepened. Her body heated as she felt his hands glide, every so lightly, along her arms.

Please, let him want me. Just for a little while, let him want me.

She dug her fingers into his arms as if for leverage, as if to keep from being swallowed up whole, leaving slight impressions in the muscles. Her head swam with hope, with excitement.

Each kiss flowered into a cluster that robbed her of her senses. Someone else would have said she was crazy, leaving herself open this way to a man she knew didn't love her. A man who could only break her heart in the end.

But it wasn't the end she was thinking about. It was the moment. And the way he could make her blood churn and ignite.

Connor tugged at the ends of her blouse, pulling them out of the waistband of her skirt. Very slowly, his lips still on hers, he slipped his hands beneath her shirt, touching her waist. He felt her bare skin quicken. Tremble. Something within him quickened, as well, responding. Glorying.

This wasn't right, he upbraided himself. If he had a shred of decency in him, he'd stop now, before he let this go too far.

It had already gone too far.

His hunger for her had gone too far. And his desire for her had gone too far. As for decency, it found itself outnumbered by demands of the flesh that were far stronger. It might have been possible to do the right thing if she hadn't melted like cotton candy on his tongue when he'd brought his mouth to hers. If her lips hadn't been so willing, her body so soft, her kisses so eager. He'd taken a young, virginal girl the first time. This time it was a woman who returned his ardor, and she was too much for him to resist.

With every pass of his lips against hers, every sigh that echoed in his brain, every ache that throbbed within his body, Connor sped further and further from the right thing and streaked like a bullet toward the only thing.

In his feverish brain, he kept hearing a fragment of refrain from an old song, something about if loving her was wrong, then he didn't want to be right. More than anything else in the world, he wanted to make love with Lacy tonight.

Over and over again, Lacy relived the first night he'd taken her. That night she'd found him, sitting in his room, lost and alone. Her heart had broken to see him like that, and when he'd turned to her for solace, she'd given it and herself freely. The single night was almost two years in the past. She'd clung to it all this time. Even when she'd had amnesia, somewhere deep in the night, silvery pieces of the memory would come back to her. Haunting her. Making her long to return to the life she'd lost, if only to find the man who had made her feel this way.

And now he was here. Wanting her. Making her head spin as he stood with her in the living room, stealing her breath. Claiming her heart.

With hands not quite steady, she unbuttoned his shirt and splayed her fingertips along his bare chest. She could hear his sudden intake of breath. Could feel his desire flaring. Triumph thundered in her veins, sending her to the next level.

A single salvo of guilt pierced him, and he struggled to rally around it. Decency was making a last, enfeebled stand. He drew his head back, trying to focus on her face. It swam before him, beautiful, still as innocent as the morning dew.

"Lacy, maybe we shouldn't—"

Unlike the first time, when she could only follow where he led her, this time she was his equal. She knew exactly what she wanted and exactly what it would cost her.

On her toes, she brought her lips to his. "Maybe we should," she whispered against them.

It was all he needed. Any aspirations he had toward sainthood crashed and burned with those three words. With all his heart, he wished he were stronger or that there would be no regrets for her, but wishing was for children, and he had long ceased to be one. There would be regrets, a host of them. But they were for morning.

And the night was here now.

Slipping his hands higher on her waist, he cupped her breasts, surrendering his very soul in exchange for the look he saw in her eyes as he touched her.

She took him prisoner with her innocence, an innocence that had somehow survived despite everything. He was captivated and captured by the woman he knew, ultimately, he was wronging.

If she was his, then he was hers. For the night.

He kissed Lacy in a way he had never kissed anyone, not even her, before.

Picking her up in his arms, he carried her up the stairs to his room, his mouth sealed to hers. Instinct and familiarity brought him to his door.

Once inside the room, an eagerness sprang up within him. He freed her of her blouse, her skirt, then curbed himself as he peeled away her undergarments. He caught his breath. The last time he'd seen her like this, his mind had been hazed with grief and alcohol. Now there was nothing fogging his brain except desire. She was magnificent. And his.

The battle of right and wrong raged within his

brain, giving him no peace, even as he lost himself in the pleasures of her eager mouth, her willing body.

If her innocence captured him, her prowess closed the prison door.

Moving with instincts she had no idea she'd had, Lacy not only was made love to, but made love on her own. She matched every pass of his hands with one of her own, divesting him of his clothing just as he did her. Divesting him of any barriers that existed within his soul. His shirt fell on top of hers, his pants sank against her skirt and their undergarments, hers flimsy, his practical, were relegated to a place of their own.

Cloaked in only the moonlight streaming into the room, Lacy made herself irresistible to him.

Her fingers, so nimble, reduced a towering man to a supplicating teenager. Bringing to life responses, emotions that had long since faded from his life. She made him catch fire. It wasn't merely the stripping away of her clothes and seeing her young, supple body that transformed him from a confident male to a man who would have willingly dropped to his knees before her if she merely gave the sign. It was the confidence that radiated from her very being.

She felt so right in his arms. So right in his bed. The more he kissed her, the more he touched her, the more he wanted her until he felt as if he was on fire. And with each move he made, the bars around him closed in a little more.

Even the sound of her breathing excited him. And her eyes—her eyes seemed to look right into him. Humbling him. Igniting him.

He couldn't have turned his back on her and walked away if the ransom of the entire earth depended on it.

It was hard to keep her wits about her, to focus and not give herself up completely to the pleasures of his caress, to the fire he so skillfully stoked. But she wanted him to remember this. To lie awake in his bed and relive this night over and over again in his mind until his body was a mass of pulsing desires and needs. Until he found he wanted only her in his life.

She was determined.

But it was difficult to stay focused and determined when his lips traveled the length of her, outlining every pulse point with deep, openmouthed kisses that reduced her to a throbbing mass. When he made her body twist and turn against him, desperate for that final moment of extreme gratification.

Desperate to feel him within her.

He couldn't hold back. Not a second longer. He took what precautions he could, then, braced over her, he joined his hands to Lacy's, his eyes on hers as he slowly moved into her. He saw the flare of desire mingled with something akin to triumph. He felt the beating of her heart within his chest. Sealing his lips to hers, he began the dance that would bring the two of them to the mutual pleasure they sought at the summit's crest.

The tempo increased. He tasted his name on her lips as the muffled cry melted against his flesh. He whispered her name in his mind, softly, like a prayer.

And when it was over, there were no regrets. There was only softness and peace as, spent, Connor held her in his arms.

FLUSHED from her visit to Connor's house, Megan breezed into her kitchen through the garage. It didn't surprise her to see Harold looking as if he was waiting for her to make her entrance. The butler always seemed to materialize when he was needed. When she was a little girl, Abby used to think the man was magical. At times, Megan was inclined to believe that.

"I won't be needing anything tonight, Harold, I had a marvelous dinner at Connor's house."

"Yes, ma'am." The older man inclined his head. "But I fear there might be something Mr. Blake might need."

"Hugh?" Without thinking, she glanced at the telephone on the wall. Why was the lawyer calling? "What would he be needing?"

"Your presence, ma'am. He's waiting for you in the study. Been here since eight." Anticipating her next steps, Harold moved out of Megan's way without bothering to look. It was as if he knew what she would do next.

"Thank you, Harold." Leaving her purse for Harold to put away, Megan hurried from the room.

Had she forgotten a meeting she'd scheduled with Hugh, or was this something unexpected? Although their business association extended beyond the usual client-lawyer relations, and although over the years they had become friends, Hugh didn't usually make a habit of dropping by.

Megan pushed open the study doors. "Hugh, what are you doing here?"

Hugh Blake set down the empty glass he'd been debating filling and rose to his feet. He knew the gesture had fallen on hard times of late, chivalry being mostly out of fashion, but Megan Maitland deserved a little chivalry in his opinion, and he was more than happy to supply it.

The smile on his face was genial. "Waiting for you."

Megan crossed to the fireplace. "That much is obvious, but why?"

He didn't give her the real reason, afraid that it might shred the fabric of the friendship that had taken years to weave. Instead, he nodded at the large manila envelope on the coffee table beside his empty glass and the cut-glass decanter Harold had left with him.

"I had some contracts for your signature. A few

securities maturing, needing a turnover, things like that. Your place was on my way home, so I thought I'd drop them off instead of asking you to come down to the office. Harold decided to ply me with Scotch. Damn near melted my bones, forcing me to stick around until the effects wore off.'' He frowned, raising a brow as he looked at the decanter instead of at the woman who did more than merely melt his bones. ''Need to be stone-cold sober on the roads. With my luck, some overzealous motorcycle jockey one third my age will be hiding behind a sign, itching to get me in his radar beam. I thought it was safer to just wait it out.''

Enchanted, he watched her for a moment as she straightened a photograph on the mantel. ''All right, I've told you what I'm doing here, now it's your turn.''

Her smile illuminated her eyes, the way it always did, he thought. ''I live here, remember?''

''I meant what you were doing with your evening. You walked in with cheeks that were flushed like a young girl's.''

She moved her hand vaguely around. ''The night air's still a bit sultry.''

His brow rose a little higher. Was she seeing someone? he wondered. She'd been alone for so long. ''You parked the car inside the garage, and unless the last hurricane has disengaged it from the house, you entered via the side door—which is completely enclosed.''

Amusement deepened her smile. ''I wasn't aware that Sherlock Holmes was seeking a successor.'' She'd known Hugh Blake most of her adult life, known him when his hair was the color of sun-kissed gold instead of silver. He'd been William's lawyer when she'd met him. Over the years, he'd become her confidant as well as her lawyer. She felt she didn't have a truer friend in the world. ''I had dinner with Connor and Lacy.''

Unconsciously, Hugh squared his broad shoulders. She'd trusted him with her secret long before she'd made her announcement. It had been a shock, though he hadn't said anything. It had struck him at the time as amazing that he could know someone for so long and yet not truly know them at all. He'd struggled to picture the young girl, pregnant and abandoned by the man she loved, and had difficulty reconciling that to the woman he saw before him. What had intervened was a strong, steely band of jealousy he hadn't realized he was capable of. Jealousy that there had been someone who had swept her off her feet so completely that she had surrendered herself to him without a qualm.

But he had gotten his reaction under control swiftly, showing nothing but dependable understanding. It wasn't his place to be anything else. He'd advised her to pick her time carefully before dropping her bombshell. The Maitland children were a good, decent lot, but they would need time to adjust. It surprised him how quickly they had all come to terms with this part of their mother's past.

Far better than he had, he mused. "What restaurant did you go to? The new one I suggested?" He'd made the suggestion, hoping to take her there himself, but at the last minute had changed his mind, not wanting to change the status quo between them.

She shook her head. "The new ranch."

Feeling suddenly tired, Megan crossed to the sofa and sat down, patting the spot beside her as she turned her eyes to Hugh. He joined her.

"You should see what Lacy's done with the place. The girl is an absolute marvel. The sooner Connor comes around and realizes that, the happier they'll both be."

She was matchmaking, he realized. It didn't surprise him. He knew that Megan believed that she took a hands-off approach to her children's lives whenever possible, but quite the opposite was true.

He wasn't in the mood to talk about Connor. His attention was focused elsewhere. On the years that had gone by, wasted. "And you?"

She didn't see the connection. "And me what?"

He tried to ignore how close he was to her. How much he wanted to be even closer. He stayed inside his role as the reliable family friend and lawyer, even though there were times the role threatened to choke off his very air. "What would it take to make you happier?"

She didn't even pause to consider. There was no need. "I'm already happy. I have all my children, finally, around me. I have grandchildren, my work."

"I said happier, not happy."

His eyes touched hers, and for a moment, just a moment, something stirred within her. She told herself she was being absurd. What she was feeling was a product of fatigue. "If I were any happier, I might just become airborne."

He laughed softly. "Well, we wouldn't want that to happen, now, would we?" Because they were old friends, because he had held her hand during crisis after crisis and been there for her when William had died, as she had been there for him when Elaine had passed on, Hugh leaned over and kissed her temple. Anything more would have been out of line. "I think the effects of this glass of Scotch have worn off. I'll be by your office in a couple of days to pick those up." He nodded at the manila envelope. "No hurry, really."

She didn't understand. "Then why did you stop by?"

Because, quite simply, he'd wanted to see her. Just to see her, to catch a whiff of the scent she always wore, nothing more. "I was feeling a little nostalgic. This is our fortieth anniversary. Well, not ours, exactly, but it's been forty years since I began working for the Maitlands.''

"Forty years?" Such a long time. It should make her feel old. Yet oddly enough she felt very young tonight. Younger than usual. "Today?"

He nodded. "Forty years. Today."

She rose to get another glass from the bar. "I'd say that deserves a toast.''

He shifted in his seat, watching her. Enjoying the way it felt seeing her approach him. "If I have another glass, I'll have to stay another half hour." And then he smiled as he moved his glass toward the decanter. "Fill the glass, Megan." He watched her pour a little of the Scotch into his glass, then her own. "Oh, by the way, you might be happy to hear that Janelle's arraignment is coming up day after tomorrow.''

The news caught her off guard. She set the decanter down. "Find out the time. I want to be there."

Megan never ceased to amaze him. Another woman would have avoided all contact with trash like Janelle Davis. "What in heaven's name for, Megan? That she-devil put you through hell."

Megan took a deep breath. "Yes, she did. But that she-devil is also my niece. By marriage."

"You're joking." But he saw that she wasn't. Hugh scowled. This was something he should have known. It wasn't often he was caught by surprise professionally. "Are you sure?"

Megan pressed her lips together. "Positive."

He wanted evidence. "How do you know?"

"Jake found out through a fingerprint check, but he kept the news from me until after Chase was rescued. And Lacy did her own search. She took it upon herself to check it out for me. On Chelsea's computer. I told you the girl was resourceful. I think Connor's underestimating her." She could see by the look in Hugh's eyes that he had little interest in Connor's thoughts at the moment. "Lacy traced birth and death certificates issued in Nevada."

"Nevada?"

"That's where Janelle's from. Lacy is completely convinced that the information is authentic and that Janelle is my late brother-in-law Robert's oldest daughter from his second marriage." She picked up her glass.

He did the same. More twists and turns. Hugh shook his head as he raised his glass. "No wonder you keep me around. Can't identify the players without a scorecard of some sort. I'll look into this further for you."

"No need. I have Max doing a little more research on that lost branch of the family." She saw her answer disappoint Hugh. Laughing, Megan looked into his eyes. "And to address your last statement, Hugh, I 'keep you around' for a great many more reasons than just sorting out the players for me." She raised her glass. "To another forty years."

"To another forty years," he echoed, touching the rim of his glass to hers. For now, it was all he could ask for.

CONNOR TOOK LACY not once, but three times that night. Each time he did, he waited for satisfaction to come, to blanket him and let his body relax. But it never came. Instead, each time an even deeper craving would possess him, driving him on until finally he catapulted over the edge of exhaustion. All he could manage was to cradle Lacy against him in his bed, praying she would find it in that beautiful heart of hers to forgive him someday.

He wasn't aware of the sigh that escaped his lips.

She raised her head slightly to look at him. "What?"

He smiled, surprised he had enough energy for even that. "You wear me out, Lacy."

He felt her hair brushing along his arm as she shifted, turning into him. "I was going to say the same thing about you."

His smile deepened, ripening in affection. There were different definitions of being worn out. "Yeah, but at your age—"

He got no further. Raising herself up on her elbow, she pressed her finger to his lips.

"Shh. We're not going to bring that awful subject up. Age has nothing to do with it. Except maybe when it comes to experience." She cocked her head, her smile warming him, her confidence exciting him. Was he losing his mind? He was on the brink of complete meltdown—how could he want her again? ''And your experience was wonderful.''

But he did want her.

He could have devoured her. So exhausted that even drawing a breath was a chore, he still could have eaten her up whole. Raising his head, he caught her bottom lip in his mouth and sucked it just enough to see the sparks entering her eyes again.

Now he'd done it, he thought.

And he was glad.

THE BED was empty when she woke sometime before dawn. The smile that had risen even in sleep disappeared from her lips as she felt the sheets. They were cool. He'd left the bed a while ago.

The warm glow that had encased her body since last night faded into the darkness. With a sigh, she got out of bed and began slipping on the clothes that had been discarded in the heat of passion.

Lacy shivered.

Well, what had she expected? She knew this wasn't going to be a walk in the park. There was no way she could change Connor O'Hara. He was what he was. Confusing, but honorable for all that.

She both respected and damned him for it.

Dressed, she reminded herself that she had a little boy who needed her. It helped fill in the gaping holes. But not completely.

CHAPTER TWELVE

SHE HADN'T EXPECTED to feel anything.

Especially not this strange, pervading sadness. Janelle especially hadn't thought she'd feel this way about Petey.

But she did.

When the dust had settled, when it had become clear that the plan she had been nurturing more carefully than most mothers nurtured their firstborn was disintegrating before her eyes, Janelle's immediate reaction had been anger. She'd screamed like a banshee, hurling obscenities at the men who had surrounded them and snatched victory out of her well-manicured fingers.

Petey's being shot after he'd fired at the men had only registered on the distant fringes of her mind. Hardly worth notice. Even later, when she was told that he was dead, his death was just a part of the whole, a troublesome detail, at best.

But as she lay in her cell at night, watching the shadows recede and extend in some mysterious, eternal game of tag, it had come to her. Penetrated her consciousness, then the barricaded walls of her inner self.

Petey was dead.

His had been a pitiful life, an expendable life, of little or no consequence to anyone but Petey, she supposed. But he had loved her in his own way and done as she'd asked, allowing himself to be manipulated. Manipulated to death.

His death bothered her. And gradually, gnawing away at the layers with which she'd learned, from an early age, to insulate herself from the rest of the world, it came to upset her. So much so that it began to prey on her mind, haunting her.

As she entered the courtroom, buffered by two formidable prison matrons, Janelle's eyes quickly took account of the people seated in the rows behind the gate that separated the accused from the accusers, searching for her husband's murderers. Never mind that only one had pulled the trigger, they were all responsible, damn them.

Especially that mealymouthed poor excuse for a woman, Lacy Clark.

Looking at the sea of faces, Janelle found her. Her eyes locked with Lacy's.

She swore to herself on the grave she hadn't been able to look at with her own eyes, her husband's grave, that she was going to find a way to avenge his death if it was the last thing she ever did.

She was going to get Lacy.

JANELLE'S EYES were burning holes into her.

It seemed like a stupid thing to feel, and yet Lacy couldn't describe it any other way. She shifted slightly, as if to find a hiding place from the heat without seeming to give Janelle the upper hand. She wasn't afraid of the other woman anymore.

Raising her chin, Lacy met Janelle's gaze head on, knowing that to do anything less would be cowardly. Worse, it would let Janelle believe she still had power over Lacy. She didn't. Those days were long gone. Along with the frightened, foolish girl she'd been, thinking that Janelle was her only friend when all along Janelle had been her only enemy. Plotting to steal her baby so she would have some sort of hold over the Maitlands.

As if a baby could be used for something so awful. If she'd had any doubts about her condemnation of Janelle, they were wiped away when she realized the woman was not above using an innocent infant for her own gain. Janelle had kidnapped Chase; she had tried to steal him not once, but twice.

The woman needed to be put away where she could never hurt Chase again. And Lacy intended to do whatever it took to see that it happened.

"If you want to leave, just say the word." Connor leaned over and whispered in her ear.

Lacy didn't look at him, afraid he might see the remnants of weakness in her eyes. Afraid he might see other things, as well. She slowly moved her head from side to side, indicating that there was no need to go. On the contrary, she was determined to stay to see this phase through, just as she was determined to see every phase through until the prison door finally slammed shut on Janelle.

She clasped her hands in her lap, holding tightly onto herself. The one person she knew she could always count on, no matter what.

In a way, Lacy was still rather surprised that Connor had volunteered to bring her to the courtroom. They had exchanged very few words since the night before last. She'd tried to pretend nothing had happened, knowing he preferred it that way. Knowing that for him, perhaps nothing had. It was only for her that the earth had moved a little, tilted on its axis and sent her spinning into the stratosphere.

But she'd come to terms with that. If she was guilty of hanging onto a small hope that somehow she could make him want her so much that all the other barriers would forever melt away, she'd certainly known better in the morning when she'd found him gone, not just from his bed but from the ranch, as well. The foremen he'd hired had said he was away for the day on business.

She'd known some of that business involved avoiding her. The tiny glimmers of hope she'd gathered to herself the night before had disappeared. Daylight had a way of tearing holes through the tissue paper dreams were made of. She was adult enough to deal with what had happened without making him uncomfortable in her presence. When he'd returned to the ranch at the end of the day, she'd greeted him with a hot meal and a few words of welcome, then gotten out of his way.

Lacy knew he'd want to be in court to make sure the woman who had tried to destroy his life would be forced to stand trial and be incarcerated for a long time. What she hadn't thought was that he'd offer to bring her with him.

Her mouth curved ever so slightly. *Offer* wasn't quite the word that applied. *Ordered* was more like it.

She'd been prepared to drive herself to the courthouse after leaving Chase at the Maitland Maternity day-care center with Beth. Connor had intercepted her at the front door, informing her that he was driving her in. There had been no room for argument, so she didn't try. If the truth were known, she was relieved that he'd taken charge. Her brave front only went so far.

Now he was sitting beside her like a sentry guarding her from harm. Maybe a small part of him did care, Lacy thought, if only because she was the mother of his child. She wouldn't push for more than that.

''Are you sure?'' he asked, the words barely audible. There was a glint of concern in his eyes as they washed over her.

"I'm sure," she replied just as the bailiff moved forward, announcing the arrival of the presiding judge.

They'd drawn Judge Angela Jennings, a stately, statuesque woman who stood six-one in her stocking feet and had raised five children on her own after the untimely death of the only man she had ever loved. Highly respected for her rulings and her integrity, she was as impartial and fair-minded a judge as they could have hoped for.

All the Maitlands had wanted to come. Those without commitments had, along with a good representation of their friends. As Lacy looked around, it appeared that no one had come to support Janelle.

They all rose in a single wave at the bailiff's behest. The judge walked in. They sat when she instructed them to do so.

Lacy held her breath as the arraignment began.

To Lacy, it was one huge blur.

It was over almost before it began. There was a preponderance of evidence, far more than necessary to convince even the most lenient of judges that Janelle Davis did indeed appear to be the one who had kidnapped Chase O'Hara, not to mention her attempt to defraud the Maitland family of a considerable amount of money by presenting them with a bogus Connor O'Hara. Without anyone to arrange for her bail, Janelle was remanded to the custody of the court and sent to jail to await her trial.

The moment the gavel came down they were on their feet, surging around Megan, who had sat beside Connor. Relieved, Megan invited everyone over to the house for dinner.

Connor struggled with the desire to retreat, knowing that to turn his mother down so soon after the tender shoots of their new beginning had poked their heads through the ground would only hurt Megan's feelings. And he supposed it wouldn't really do any harm to retreat into the family lair and absorb the support everyone so freely offered. So he'd agreed, and he and Lacy had gone to the family mansion after they'd stopped to pick up the baby.

Lacy didn't remember what she ate even while she was eating it. All she knew was that it felt particularly insulating, being in the midst of his family like this. They all seemed to care so much for one another, she thought, watching them.

And seemed bent, to a person, on making Connor feel welcomed and loved. And more, to make him realize that he had the power of a family backing him all the way.

He still didn't realize how lucky he was, Lacy thought. But he would, she felt confident. In time. The power of the love she saw around her was stronger than any loner tendencies Clarise O'Hara might have instilled in her adopted son.

In some cases, Lacy thought, love did win out.

"You look exhausted."

She jumped, nearly spilling the untouched drink she was holding. Jake had poured a glass and handed it to her more than half an hour ago, but she couldn't seem to make herself drink it. Every time she brought it near her lips, her stomach began to churn. The smell of it was responsible, which was odd—she usually wasn't sensitive to smells.

Lacy hadn't expected Connor to come up behind her.

"I am a little tired," she admitted. More than she should have been. But then, she mused, she was probably emotionally drained.

She looked pale, Connor thought, and wondered if he should have insisted that she remain at home. She didn't need to be subjected to the likes of Janelle any more than she absolutely had to. "Why don't I take you home?"

Home. It had such a nice sound. If only it really was her home. But she knew better.

It was Connor's home and her place to stay. Temporarily, until she could come up with a better situation that would allow Connor instant access to his son. She knew they couldn't go on this way indefinitely. Not without things coming to a head or getting completely out of hand.

She thought about the other night. Maybe things already were out of hand. She supposed it depended on a person's definition of out of hand.

"I don't want to be any trouble." She looked at

Ellie, sitting on the sofa. One of Megan's twin daughters, Ellie was bouncing Chase on her knee while several members of the family stood around her, talking and looking on. Chase was laughing with glee, the obvious star of the show. "I'll just take Chase and call a cab."

"I said I'll take you home." Embarrassed, Connor realized his voice had an edge to it. Muttering something under his breath, he forced himself to sound more at ease. "Besides, I'm kind of bushed myself."

He did look a little tired, she thought. Or maybe he was using her as an excuse to get away. She felt too drained to protest.

"All right." She put down the untouched glass of champagne. The light rippled through it. "Let me just say goodbye to your mother."

He slipped an arm around her shoulders, briefly securing her position beside him before he went to get their son. "I already said our goodbyes. She was the one who suggested I take you home."

Searching the other woman out, Lacy saw her by the fireplace, talking to her attorney. It struck her what a nice pair they made. She wondered if either of them realized it.

As if by instinct, Megan turned her head toward her. Their eyes met across the room, and Lacy nodded at the matriarch, who smiled and waved her on her way.

Connor returned holding Chase in his arms. He

looked so much more at ease with his son than he had a few weeks ago. Practice makes perfect, Lacy thought.

"I'll take him." She held out her arms, but Connor made no attempt to transfer possession of the little boy. Instead, he carefully shifted the child to his shoulder.

"That's okay. I've got him."

The perfect father, she thought with a smile. Connor was coming along nicely.

A sea of goodbyes accompanied them out the front door. Lacy braced herself as they went out, grateful that at least the humidity was low these past few days. The daytime temperatures were high, but not unpleasantly so, and the air cooled down by evening.

They walked in companionable silence to his car. Connor had insisted on parking the vehicle outside rather than in the garage. No doubt for a quick getaway, she thought, amused.

Lacy was all set to help Connor strap Chase into his car seat, but he did it himself. She got into the front seat and strapped herself in. Pretty soon he would be fine with Chase by himself, she thought. He had already changed a couple of diapers, and he'd fed the baby more than once.

This was what she had wanted, Lacy reminded herself. To get Connor to interact with his son. Why did triumph come with an ache?

She felt too tired to think it through. Lacy stared

at the mansion as he pulled away. There were lights on everywhere. It made her feel warm.

"I guess that's round one," Lacy murmured. Connor spared her a silent, quizzical look as he turned the vehicle around and began heading for the open road. "The arraignment," she clarified. "It's round one."

"It's just the warmup," he corrected. "The first day of the trial will be round one."

The trial promised to be a long, drawn-out affair. Chelsea had warned them of that. The local media were hungry for some angle to play up, and Maitland was a name that everyone knew. Lacy wondered how all this was going to affect Connor and if she was going to have an inkling of his reactions. He played everything so close to the chest. She supposed that was why she was so grateful when she saw him opening up to their son.

The trees that lined the road looked bigger in the night, their leafy branches reaching into the sky. "Do you know who Janelle is going to get to defend her?"

He shook his head. It hadn't crossed his mind. As far as he was concerned, they could lock the woman up and throw away the key. "She has no money, as far as anyone knows. More than likely, the court'll have to appoint someone." They came to a red light, and he eased to a stop. Connor tried to read the expression on Lacy's face. It looked like pity, but he couldn't believe he was right. Not after all that had happened. "What is it?"

Lacy shrugged self-consciously, turning her face away. "Nothing."

A month ago, he would have left it alone, grateful that she didn't want to elaborate. But things had changed between them—and within him. "Something's on your mind. What is it?"

She knew he wouldn't like this. That he'd probably get annoyed with her. But he'd asked, pressed, really, so she had no choice but to tell him. "I feel sorry for her."

Stunned, Connor pulled over to the side of the road and looked at her incredulously. "Are you out of your mind?"

There was a time the question would have intimidated her and made her back away. But that time had passed. She looked at him and shrugged again. "Maybe." But her tone said she didn't think so.

What was going on in her head? "Lacy, that woman tried to kill you. *Would* have killed you if she hadn't been frightened away by the sound of people approaching. She lied to my mother, to the whole family. She tried to get away with a huge chunk of the family money, and worst of all, she kidnapped Chase. She probably would have killed him, given half a chance, if things didn't look as if they were going to work out her way."

He waited for an answer. What the hell was Lacy

thinking, feeling sorry for a creature like that, a woman who had absolutely no conscience, no qualms about using people. She hadn't even given any indication she cared that her husband had been killed.

Lacy knew all about the attempt on her life, and the other charges, as well. Connor was only repeating details she remembered.

"I know, I know." Frustrated, she blew out a breath. It would be easy to hate Janelle. Easy if she wasn't cursed with the ability to empathize with even the cruelest of people. But she did have that ability, and it nagged at her now. Yes, Janelle had done all those hateful things, but she was alone. With no one to take her side. No one to care what happened to her. "But she just must feel so alone right now, so desperate. Her husband's dead—"

Damn it, the woman had too big a heart. It blinded her to the fact that some people were just plain irredeemable. "Petey was nothing more than a convenience for her. A means to an end. I didn't see her shed a single tear."

"Maybe nobody did." She looked at him significantly. "But some people are too proud to cry or show that they're hurt."

"You're giving the woman too much credit, Lacy. Some people are just bad to the bone. She's one of them."

Lacy sighed as he started the car again. "I suppose you're right."

"Of course I'm right." He guided the vehicle onto the road. There weren't many cars out at this time of night. He glanced at her again. So this was what pure goodness was, bottled in a beautiful vessel. Guilt and longing tugged at him from opposite sides. "Your trouble, Lacy, is that your heart is just too big."

It got in the way at times, maybe, but she didn't see it as a problem, exactly. She looked at his rigid profile and knew that he did.

"And that's a bad thing?"

"Yes," he said firmly, "it is. For you."

Although, as far as the rest of the world went, he had to admit it was rather comforting to know there was someone out there who could forgive so readily, could be so charitable.

Lacy pressed her lips together. "I already know that," she said quietly.

She was talking about them, he thought. He knew he should leave well enough alone and continue with this charade they were playing, avoid talking about the other night until it became a distant memory.

But part of him didn't think it ever would become a distant memory. And she'd been through so much already. He couldn't stand to hear the hurt in her voice. No matter how much she tried to mask it, it was still there. And he knew he was the cause of it.

Damned if I do and damned if I don't, Connor thought.

When he reached the outskirts of the city, he pressed down on the accelerator. It was now or never. "About the other night, Lacy..."

She turned her head slowly, her eyes catching his. "If you apologize to me, Connor, if you make any excuse at all, your family's going to have to be attending another trial, because I swear I won't be held responsible for what I do to you."

She looked so serious for a second that he wasn't sure what to say. And then, very slowly, a smile began to tug on his lips as he backed away from the subject, relieved to be spared this way.

"All right, Lacy. Point taken."

CHAPTER THIRTEEN

THE NEED to apologize to her stayed with Connor all
the way home despite what he'd said to Lacy in the
car. It hovered about his mind as she put Chase down
for the night.

It would be simpler to let it go, the way she'd
suggested. But he wasn't interested in simpler. He
was interested in right. He wanted to make her understand that it was only an act of weakness on his
part that had made him take her to his bed. Connor
wanted her to know that she had nothing to worry
about. It wasn't going to happen again.

When she finally came out of Chase's room, he
was waiting for her in the hall. When he said her
name, she looked up, startled.

"You look as white as a sheet." He turned her
toward the light to make sure he wasn't imagining
it. "What's the matter?"

Self-conscious, Lacy shrugged away his concern.
The nausea was passing. It was probably something
she'd eaten. "My stomach's feeling a little out of
kilter, that's all."

He didn't believe her. The apology was temporarily shelved. Connor had his own theory about why she looked as pale as she did.

"It wouldn't have anything to do with being in the courtroom today, would it?" There was a touch of sarcasm in his voice.

He'd seen the way Janelle had looked at her, had seen the malevolence in the other woman's eyes. If there hadn't been guards between them and other people to intervene, Janelle would have had no qualms about snuffing out Lacy's life.

Lacy knew what he was thinking as plainly as if it was written on a chalkboard. She unconsciously raised her chin.

"No," she insisted, "it wouldn't. I'm not afraid of her anymore, Connor. I was once," she admitted, "but not anymore."

She made him think of a bantamweight contender entering the ring with nothing to lose and everything to gain. The thought made him smile. "Tough guy, eh?"

She didn't know if he was teasing her or mocking her. In either case, the answer was the same. "No, just a tougher woman." Lacy rocked a little on the balls of her feet. "A better, new, improved me."

He couldn't resist toying with the strand of hair that curled into her face, caressing her cheek. "There was nothing wrong with the old you."

Pleasure spread through her like the rays of the early morning sun along the darkened desert. "I think that's the first time you've ever given me a compliment that didn't involve my cooking.''

"It shouldn't have been." Damn it, he upbraided himself, he was getting sidetracked again. He shouldn't be giving her compliments now—but he wanted to. Frustrated with his inability to stay on track, Connor sighed. "Which is part of the problem."

She tried to guess what was on his mind, and this time she failed. "I wasn't aware that there was a problem or that it came in parts."

He had no more finesse now than he'd had earlier. He had no choice but to plunge ahead. "Lacy, about the other night..."

She wasn't going to listen, wasn't going to have him tell her that he regretted it, that it would never happen again. That they were employer and employee, tied together by something a little more than a weekly paycheck. She knew all that, but hearing it only made it worse. Made it painful.

With effort, she masked her vulnerability with humor. It was her only weapon.

"Ah, I see that my threat in the car seems to have fallen on deaf ears." She drew herself up, a twig to his oak. "Just because I'm smaller than you doesn't mean I don't know how to physically damage you, Connor."

The very thought of her being able to inflict any sort of bodily harm to him, let alone the kind that had consequence, made him laugh. Hard. Regaining control of himself, Connor leaned on her shoulder for support. "I'm sorry, I didn't mean to laugh at you, but you don't exactly have me quaking in my boots."

"Well, you should be," she countered, although the corners of her mouth had turned up in response to his laughter. "I've learned a few things about taking care of myself since I last lived in your house."

Shelby had seen to that. The owner of the diner where she'd worked until moving into Connor's house had taken her under her wing and had become her best friend. Everyone knew her story, that she'd been assaulted and left for dead in the alley. It had been Shelby who had insisted that she take martial arts lessons so she could take care of herself.

There was no doubt in Connor's mind that Lacy had learned a few things since she'd lived at his other ranch. Learned more than a few things. The other night had proved it.

He felt his body heating at the memory.

Because he needed to touch her, he shoved his hands into his back pockets. Touching her would lead to other things, and he didn't want that.

Or so he had to believe.

"I'm sure you have," he said. "Lacy, what I'm trying to say—badly—is that I just want you to know that I won't be taking advantage of you again."

About to open the door to her room, she stopped

and turned to stare at him. Is that what he thought? Hadn't he been there the other night?

"You didn't take anything, Connor. There was no theft of any sort involved in the other night or the night that you first made love to me." Then it had been to, not with, because he'd been her first and she'd had no experience to show her the way. But it had been different the other night. They'd been equals. Which was why his apology rankled. "Taking would indicate that something was stolen from me. Nothing was. I was given something. I had nothing taken from me." She could see by the look in his eyes that he was unconvinced. That he was determined to wear that damned hair shirt and atone for his sin when there'd been no sin at all. "Can't you get that through that thick skull of yours?" As her anger rose, so did her voice. "You didn't take advantage of me. You didn't take anything. I gave it to you, without any strings of any sort."

Anger suited her. She was nothing short of magnificent. And he wanted her all over again.

As if to hold her at arm's length, he caught her by the shoulders. "Damn it, Lacy, how is it that I can have the noblest of intentions and you can blow them completely all to hell just by looking at me with those big blue eyes of yours?"

She grinned, lacing her arms around his neck, no longer tired. No longer sleepy. His hands dropped from her shoulders. "Just lucky, I guess."

She was doing it to him again, warming him with her gaze, making him want her even when he knew it was wrong. As wrong now as it had been the other night.

As wrong as it had been almost two years ago. Why couldn't he have more willpower than a debaucher locked in a wine cellar when it came to her?

Even as he asked the question, Connor felt himself weakening. "You know where this is going to lead, don't you?"

Her eyes danced as they washed over the rugged planes of his face. "No, but I have my hopes."

For her sake, he struggled. It was definitely not for his own, because for his sake, he would have taken her right there, in the hallway, nine feet away from their son's room.

He began to remove her arms from his neck but only made a halfhearted attempt. "Lacy, you're wasting yourself on me, you know that. You deserve to be with someone your own age."

She slowly shook her head. "I don't know anything of the kind. I don't want someone my own age."

He'd never been as idealistic as she was. Not even when he had been half her age. It made him feel humble just to have kissed her. "How do you know? You've never been with a younger man."

She raised her eyes to his, her mouth temptingly

close. "You don't have to go to hell to know what heaven is."

He felt the last of his resistance snapping. "Oh, damn it, Lacy, I'm trying to be noble here."

"Don't," she whispered, her breath tantalizing his mouth. Her eyes teased him. Tempted him. "Tell me what you want, Connor. What you really want. Right now. Right this minute." *Please let it be me.*

He could lie to her. But she'd know it. He felt as transparent to her as a pitcher of water. So he told her the truth. And sealed both their fates.

Very gently, he framed her face with his hands as if it was some exquisite photograph. Because it was. "I want you in my bed, Lacy. I want you lying beneath me, naked as the day you were born, sweaty with my sweat, crying out my name as I take you—"

Her mouth curved, feeding the smile into her eyes. "There's that word again."

"All right," he said gamely, "what do you want me to call it?"

There was no hesitation. She knew how she saw it. "Joining. As you join me. As I join you. Together. Sharing each other." The words were whispered seductively around his senses "Having each other."

He was beginning to believe a saint would have given in. "You make it so hard to be good."

"Then be bad," she said, coaxing. "Haven't you heard? Women like bad men."

"Women only *say* they like bad men." He laced

his hands around her waist. Holding her even as he should have been pushing her away. "What they want, ultimately, is bad men who are good."

She cocked her head as she looked at him. "Well, then?"

He had no choice.

She drove him to it.

And to his knees, both figuratively and, later, literally.

Unable to turn his back on what she offered so guilelessly, Connor wrapped his hand around hers and, without a word, led her to his room. Once inside, he pushed the door closed behind them.

But when he began to undress her in the dark, she placed her hands on his to still them.

Something inside tightened as disappointment skewered through him. She was calling a halt to it. His words had finally sunk in. "Come to your senses?"

"I never left them."

He could see her smile even in the moonlight. Turning from him, she switched on the lights. A dim, seductive atmosphere permeated the room with its massive, dark wooden furniture. Thrown, Connor looked at her quizzically.

Her reason was simple. "I want to see your eyes when you undress me. I want to see the way you look at me when we make love. When we join," she added, a faint smile on her lips. "I want to seal away every moment so that when I'm old and gray and living in my own little world, I can remember every detail of tonight.''

Connor tried to laugh away the seriousness of the moment, though in truth it humbled him beyond words. ''No pressure here.''

''No pressure,'' she echoed in a whisper, lightly caressing his cheek as she looked into his eyes. ''There's only me.''

''There is no only about you, Lacy.'' She was everything. The flame in his chest, the reason he woke up in the morning.

As his breath lodged in his chest, he slowly lifted the edge of the pale green sweater she wore and drew it up, over her head and her arms. Savoring every moment, every fraction of an inch of skin that was exposed.

Without a glance in its direction, he discarded the garment. Connor was completely captivated by the swell of her breasts directly above the white lacy demi-bra she wore.

Lacy's blood churned as he pressed his lips first to one breast, then the other, before releasing the clasp at her back. The cups slowly slid away from her.

She could feel her excitement heightening as she saw desire flare in his eyes, eyes that seemed to caress her.

Eager not to be passive, she tugged at his shirt,

releasing buttons from their holes and sending material away from his shoulders.

She wanted to feel his warm skin against hers, wanted to revel in the contact.

Held within the hypnotic gaze of his eyes, hers began to drift shut as she felt his hands skim along her curves, drawing her skirt away.

For a second, she held her breath, and her fingers froze as she drank in the delicious sensations swirling madly through her, playing a wicked game of tag. And then she remembered what she was about and unnotched his belt, pulling the leather from the metal loop. Coaxing the zipper down to its source.

She felt his desire harden as she tugged away first the denim, then the cotton.

The next moment, nude, Lacy felt herself being propelled backward. She fell onto the bed, landing beneath him.

After that, it was difficult to recall the order of things. One sensation mushroomed into another, battering her body, echoing the movement of his hands, his lips, his body as he caressed, explored, anointed and generally turned her into a pulsating mass of needs that centered around him.

His hands and lips were everywhere, finding all of her erotic points, creating new ones. She discovered that the backs of her knees were incredibly susceptible to his sensual assault. As were the insides of her elbows. And as for her abdomen...

He left her almost mindless. Mindless and yet insatiably greedy for every shred of pleasure he could give her. Desperate to do the same to him. To make him want her the way she wanted him. To make him quiver at the hint of her lips on his flesh.

When he brought his mouth to the very core of her being, initiating her in all the pleasures that could be, she felt the urge to both scramble toward the wave that drenched her and pull away from it, wanting to draw the sensation out as long as possible, yet greedy for its culmination.

Spent, she struggled to rally. It couldn't be one-sided. It couldn't. He needed to be made to feel the way she did.

Lacy moved against him, coaxing his body close to hers. She heard him moan as she slid her hand between their bodies and touched him. A sense of empowerment washed over her.

Tangled together, they did their best to please each other. To share the sensations they felt, offering them like gifts to each other. Like silent pledges they had no right to make, but made just the same, because it was impossible not to.

Impossible not to offer their hearts, however mutely, to each other.

He came to her slowly, sheathed, protected, ever mindful of her. Drawing out each second, turning it into a lifetime.

As if a lifetime would even be one-tenth enough to show her what she meant to him.

Right and wrong ceased to have meaning. There was only here, only now. Only her.

As he filled her, she filled him. With so many wondrous feelings it was impossible to identify them all. All he could do was enjoy them.

And pray that the dawn never came.

She found it hard to catch her breath. It was snatched away at the final moment as his lips pressed against hers, as his heart beat wildly against her own.

Gasping, she drew back and realized that somehow, this time, she had managed to be the one on top. Now, without an ounce of energy to her name, she melted against him, her legs splayed around his like flesh and blood parentheses, her oxygen-depleted lungs heaving against his broad, muscular chest, her fingers limp in his hair as her hair curtained one of his shoulders.

"Tired?" His question skimmed the top of her head.

At first, all she could offer in response was a languorous sound. And then, from somewhere, words finally came. "This would be a very bad time to hold a fire drill," she murmured against his chest.

Her breathing tickled his skin.

His arm tightened around her. She'd surprised him. Again. The woman had shared with him pure erotic sex at the end, and yet it was somehow still tinged with a sweetness that wrenched his very soul.

He knew at that moment that he would never be able to get his fill of her. No matter how exhausted he became, he would continue to want her, to want to make love with her.

"Then we won't hold one," he told her.

Though it wasn't easy, she summoned the strength to raise her head. Blinking, she focused her eyes enough to look at him. Humor painted a smile on her lips. "Promise?"

He tried to sound solemn and had no idea if he failed miserably or succeeded. "Promise."

She laid her head down, content to remain here like this, being held by him. Wishing she could stay like this indefinitely.

"I'll hold you to that."

"Uh-huh." He wasn't sure if he said it or just thought it. Connor concentrated on making his mouth work. "And I'll just hold you."

He felt her smile as it widened against his chest. "I'd like that."

"Yeah, me, too."

Connor remained that way a long time, just holding her to him. Vaguely aware that the minutes were passing, transforming into hours. It didn't matter. There was nowhere else he wanted to be. Only here. With her.

He'd never known such contentment.

But he wasn't a fool. He knew he was living in a fool's paradise and that soon, all too soon, he'd be forced to evacuate and stand helplessly by as the locks were changed on the doors, barring his entry.

She murmured something in her sleep. He tried to hear what it was, but it was too soft. Probably nothing, he knew. But he'd still wanted to hear.

He was too old for her, he thought, and she'd realize that soon enough, when the novelty of their affair wore off.

There was nothing else he could classify it as in his mind. An affair. To think of it as anything more would be to feed himself false hopes, and he had never been guilty of that.

Above all else, Connor knew he had to stay grounded. The reality was that Lacy would find a younger man to love her all too soon. A younger man whose stamina promised to last years before it eroded.

A younger man who could grow old with her, not before her.

But for now, he could just lie here, holding Lacy to him, listening to her breathe. And pretend that what they had would continue forever.

CHAPTER FOURTEEN

THERE WAS no doubt in her mind.

Though a single test hadn't been done to support her suspicions, Lacy knew the signs. Remembered them well from the last time.

A bittersweet sadness pervaded her. All it had taken then was once.

All it had taken this time was once, too. By her calculations, it had happened the first night, after Megan had come to dinner and then gone home.

She was pregnant.

They'd used protection, and still she'd gotten pregnant. She knew these things happened, but the odds were supposed to have been in her favor.

They weren't.

Standing with the cool tile pressing against her bare feet in the bathroom whose renovations she had so carefully oversaw, Lacy felt tears gathering in her eyes.

This couldn't be happening. Not again. Not unplanned.

Although she already loved this unborn child forming beneath her heart, she couldn't help feeling that it simply wasn't fair. This would push her further away from Connor instead of closer.

She couldn't tell him about this, couldn't stand to see him stoically accept this newest addition into their lives. She wanted happiness, and there wouldn't be any.

And what if this second unscheduled pregnancy changed the way he felt and acted toward Chase? The little boy was responding to Connor so well. Responding to his daddy. She couldn't just rob Chase of that.

So this was what she got for falling head over heels for the same man not once in her life, but three times. Three times, because she'd fallen for him as Sara, as well, when she couldn't remember anything else about herself, not even her name. But the moment she'd seen him, her heart had remembered. Without knowing who or why, it had remembered how she had felt about Connor. Remembered and opened itself up all over again.

And now she was pregnant with his child for the second time.

Lacy blinked back tears. She couldn't do this to Connor. To them. Or to Chase. Couldn't put Connor through the awkwardness of having two children with a woman he wasn't married to. And she wasn't about to put him in the position of proposing to her again.

There was only one thing she could do.

PULLING HIS HAND back from the rim of the hot fry-
ing pan, Connor stifled an oath, then quickly stuck
his hand under the faucet so cold running water
would cover the grazed area. He didn't know what
the hell he was doing, but he was trying.

He shook his head at his clumsiness. This was
completely unlike him. He'd be the first to admit it.
But it felt right just the same.

Damn, but even with his fingers smarting, he felt
like singing. Not just with his lips, where the tune
would emerge completely off-key, but with his entire
being. He felt as if he'd swallowed a six-piece band.
A band that could only play one tune, one song.

And its name was Lacy.

Part of him still knew he was living in a fool's
paradise, but after the other night, he was determined
to hang on to that paradise for as long as possible.

Maybe, if he behaved a little nicer to her, took
more care of her feelings, she wouldn't notice all the
things he knew she eventually was destined to notice.

Now was all he had, and he wanted to make the
most of it. If he didn't wind up burning his fingers
in the process.

"What's this?"

Surprised, Connor turned from the stove and saw
that Lacy was in the doorway, holding Chase. She
was earlier than he'd anticipated. He'd hoped that
she would sleep just five minutes longer. He'd
wanted to take this up to her on a tray.

The best laid plans of mice and men…

She still looked under the weather, he thought as she crossed to him. She'd had that faint pallor for at least a couple of weeks. Because he liked his privacy, he wasn't the kind to butt in on anyone else's business. But she wasn't just anyone else, she was Lacy, and he cared about her. Maybe after she'd eaten, he'd insist that she see a doctor.

Or at least suggest it.

"It's called breakfast. Or at least, it will be once I get it on the table." He pulled a plate out of the cupboard and tilted the pan, emptying its contents onto the plate. "Scrambled eggs and toast," he announced needlessly, feeling a little awkward. He dumped the pan into the sink and surrounded the yellow mound on the plate with two slices of buttered toast. "I was going to make bacon, but you're out of bacon. We're out of bacon," he corrected.

She could only stare numbly at the offering, not knowing what to think. "Why?"

He shrugged, his awkwardness mounting. She wasn't sitting down. "Because I ate the last of it the other day, I guess."

Holding Chase closer, she raised her eyes to Connor's face. "No, I mean why did you do this?"

Why did she have to ask? Couldn't she just sit down and accept the gesture? He pulled out a chair for her, waiting. "You're always cooking for me and I thought that maybe you'd like a break."

That really didn't explain anything, Lucy thought. This wasn't like him. As much as he'd softened toward her and Chase, this wasn't like him. Something was going on. "I'm being paid to cook," she said.

Helpless, he threw up his hands. "Then call it a whim." He saw her looking at the plate and thought he knew what she was thinking. It was a far cry from the breakfasts she made for him. "You might want to call it something else after you sample it," he added.

She could feel the tears gathering. Her emotions had gone completely out of whack. But no one had ever cooked for her before, not since she'd been a small girl.

"I'm sure it's very good," she said slowly, afraid her voice would crack, "I'm just not very hungry right now."

He knew it. She was sick. That was the only explanation.

Connor surprised her by placing his hand on her forehead. She tried to draw back, but his other hand was firmly on her shoulder.

"No fever." Connor frowned, dropping his hand to his side. "Maybe I should run you over to Maitland Maternity."

Her heart jumped, though she struggled not to show it. Did he suspect for some reason? Had he heard her throwing up this morning? She was sure he'd gone downstairs before she'd dragged herself into the bathroom and emptied the meager contents of her stomach.

"Why?"

He thought that was an odd question, but chalked it up to her being ill. "To see Abby. She wouldn't mind squeezing you in and taking a look at you. Maybe she could recommend a good GP for future visits."

The last thing she wanted was to see an ob-gyn, even if it was Abby. Doctor-patient privilege aside, news had a way of surfacing and traveling through the Maitland infrastructure. She'd seen evidence of that even before she'd regained her memory and discovered that Connor was part of the family. He was Abby's half brother, and that made the baby she was carrying Abby's niece or nephew.

"No." Her voice was adamant. "I'm just a little under the weather."

The circles under Lacy's eyes looked like deep smudges. He couldn't remember her ever looking this way, not even when she pulled what amounted to all-nighters with Chase.

"Under the weather, nothing." He snorted dismissively. "It looks as if the weather ran right over you driving a Mack truck."

Why did he pick now to be thoughtful? Any other time, she would have reveled in it. "I'll be all right. Really."

To prove it, she deposited Chase in his high chair,

strapped him in, then sat in the chair Connor had pulled out for her. She picked up her fork and dug in.

"Look, I'm eating, see?" The eggs had been in the pan a little longer than necessary, and the toast was burned, but it didn't matter. He'd done this for her. It was something she was going to remember for the rest of her life. She turned her face to his, smiling. "It's very good."

She was being charitable, and they both knew it. He suddenly felt like a little boy trying to impress an adult. "It's overcooked."

He began to pull the plate away from her, but she stopped him. "Just the way I like it."

Embarrassed, he turned away, pretending to be busy cleaning the pan. The man who had invented no-stick cookware deserved to be made a saint, he thought as the burned-on pieces lifted off the skillet.

"I'm going to be gone most of the day," he told her, then mentioned the foreman he'd hired the day after he'd bought the ranch. "Gus brought the new horses and—"

Was he trying to find ways to avoid her? Lacy felt as if all her emotions had booked permanent passage on a roller coaster. "You don't have to make excuses to me."

He tossed the sponge into the sink a little too hard. It bounced and landed on the counter. Why was she twisting everything? Didn't she understand he was making an all-out effort?

"I'm not making excuses, I'm just letting you know where I'll be in case you need me." That sounded too possessive. Backtracking, he shrugged. "Or something. I'll be on the north range. So if you need me—"

She nodded, anticipating his next words. "I'll send one of the hands."

"Or you can just call." He pulled a cell phone out of his back pocket. The phone was one of the concessions he'd made to progress. A man couldn't afford to be out of touch these days. "What's so funny?"

Despite the situation that was weighing so heavily on her mind, Lacy began to laugh. The image of Connor talking into a cell phone while sitting astride a horse was so incongruous it was funny.

She waved away the frown that was forming on his face. "Nothing. I'm sorry, I didn't mean to laugh. It's just that I don't think of you as a modern sort of man, that's all. To be honest, I can see you sending smoke signals more readily than talking on a cell phone." He was, and always would be, the rugged, strong, silent type to her. Cell phones didn't enter into the picture.

He looked at the phone in his hand, and his frown melted into a grin. It was kind of funny, at that, he supposed. "Just goes to show you that you don't know everything about me."

No, she thought as he turned his back on her again and finished cleaning the spatula, she didn't know everything about him. Just as he didn't know everything about her.

And she was going to keep it that way as long as possible.

THAT MORNING, after she watched Connor ride away on his palomino, Lacy got Chase ready and drove into the city. She purchased a home pregnancy kit in a pharmacy where no one knew her and brought it home with her, hiding it in her underwear drawer beneath a nightgown. She would use it the following morning. The hours until dawn promised to drag on.

Until Connor came to her room that night after she had put Chase to bed.

She'd thought he was going to work into the wee hours of the night. She'd gone to bed, leaving him to go over sales receipts and bills in his den.

When he stood in her doorway less than ten minutes later, her heart jumped.

And placed itself straight in the palm of his hand. She knew why he was there before a word was said. Silently, she crossed to him, took his hand and drew him into her room.

That night, Lacy made love with him, and to him, with wild abandonment, trying not to dwell on the thought that it was for the last time. Anticipating the positive answer to the pregnancy test, she'd made up her mind what to do. All she needed was the courage to carry out her plan.

But in the interim, she wanted this one last night. A night of love to last in Connor's memory forever, even when everything else faded away.

To last in her own after all the other dreams had disappeared.

"WELL, HI, STRANGER."

Rounding the diner's long counter, Shelby Lord threw her arms around Lacy. Chase squealed at the close contact and immediately grabbed her sleeve. With a laugh, Shelby disengaged herself from his grasping fingers.

"Strong grip," she commented. "Nobody's going to order this little guy around when he grows up." She patted her sleeve into place. In the lull between breakfast and lunch, the diner had only a couple of patrons at the counter and one in a booth. All were immersed in the newspapers they were reading. "I haven't seen you around since Connor whisked you out to his ranch." Pleasure filled Shelby's eyes as she took inventory of her friend. "How've you been?"

Lacy still felt a little shaky about the course she'd plotted for herself. She'd come to the diner because Shelby was as close a friend as she had in this world.

The bond between them had been forged when Shelby had realized Lacy needed a hand. Shelby had extended it, never once making Lacy feel as if she was obligated in any way. That was what made Shelby so special.

Lacy took a deep breath. "Well, I've been better."

Concerned, Shelby nodded to the corner booth where she usually sat observing the customers when she wasn't working behind the counter.

"Pull up a booth and tell me about it." She waited until Lacy sat with Chase on her knee. She kept her voice low, knowing that whatever was wrong, Lacy would want it to remain between the two of them. "Connor not treating you right? Because if he's not—"

Lacy shook her head. She didn't want her best friend entertaining a single bad thought about Connor. Especially since he was trying to be so nice to her. "He's treating me fine, Shelby." She pressed her lips together. "I'm the one who isn't treating him right."

She'd been right. Something *was* up. Shelby placed her hand over Lacy's, squeezing it warmly.

"That's not possible." Shelby remained silent as long as she could, waiting. When Lacy said nothing, Shelby took the lead. "Want to tell me about it, or do I have to play twenty questions?"

There was no way to say this but to blurt it out. "I'm pregnant." The instant the words tumbled from her lips, tears threatened to spill from her eyes. Lacy pressed her lips together, as if that would somehow make the tears recede.

"Lacy, that's wonderful!" And then Shelby's enthusiasm was dampened as Lacy's expression penetrated her consciousness. "I take it it's not exactly that wonderful."

Lacy drew a deep breath, then shook her head. The sympathy in Shelby's voice almost made her break down. "No."

Chase was scrunching up the paper place mat in front of him. Very gently, Shelby pulled it out of his hands to keep the mat from going into the little boy's mouth. "Have you told Connor?"

Chase began to fuss. "No." Digging through her purse, Lacy found the cookies she'd packed before she left. She opened the small bag and gave the boy one. Delighted, he gleefully began to gnaw on it.

Lacy was aware that Shelby's eyes never left her face. "Do you love him?"

There was no point in denying it. Shelby would see the truth. "Yes."

"Then tell him," Shelby insisted, leaning forward so her voice could carry emphasis without being raised. "Tell him you love him and that there's another example of that love on the way."

If only it were that easy. If only this was some kind of fairy tale with the promise of a happily ever after in the offing. But it wasn't, and the sooner she dealt with that, the better. She'd been a fool to let this go as long as it had.

"No."

For such a little thing, Lacy could be infuriatingly stubborn. "All right," Shelby declared, beginning to get up, "I'll tell him." She intended to make the call to Connor immediately.

Lacy grabbed her hand, holding her in place. "No!" One of the people at the counter looked up from the paper he was reading. Lacy pressed her lips together and lowered her voice. "No," she repeated, her voice no less urgent for the lack of volume. She saw it had no effect on Shelby. Panic began to set in. "Swear you won't tell him, Shelby. Swear."

Frustration bit a chunk out of her. "All right, all right, I swear." She blew out a breath, her anger directed at the situation rather than at Lacy. "But you're making a big mistake."

"Maybe." Part of her feared that she'd regret this. But it was for the best. "But it's mine to make."

Shelby's eyes swept over her friend's trim form. The woman looked like a size nothing right now. But that would change. "It's not like you can keep it a secret, you know. He's going to notice."

Lacy was silent, knowing she was on the cusp of another heated discussion. Shelby was going to try to talk her out of this.

"Not if I'm not around."

Shelby's mouth dropped open. "You're leaving?"

Was she out of her mind? A pregnant woman needed the support of her friends at a time like this. Especially a pregnant woman with a child.

Lacy nodded, momentarily avoiding Shelby's eyes. But that was cowardly, and she was going to require a lot of courage to carry this out. She might as well begin now. She looked at Shelby. "It's the only thing I can do. I was thinking about leaving even before this happened."

None of this made sense to Shelby. "But why, for heaven's sake?"

Lacy shared with her what she wouldn't have shared with anyone else. "Because I can't go on, day after day, loving him and not having him. Knowing that the only reason I'm there is Chase."

Shelby frowned. "He didn't put that bun in your oven because of Chase."

Lacy lifted a shoulder. She wasn't going to try to fool herself about why Connor had come to her. Why he'd made love with her. "He's only human, Shelby. And I made things easy for him."

"Right." Sarcasm twisted her mouth. "Running around without your clothes on again, were you?"

Lacy took no offense. She knew what Shelby was trying to do. Trying to shift the responsibility.

"You know what I mean."

"Yes, I do, and I think you're wrong. Give the man a chance to tell you that himself. Don't put words into his mouth. From what I hear, Janelle did

that and ruined it for both of you the first time. Don't
you be the one to ruin it this time.''

Shelby didn't understand, Lacy thought. She
wasn't ruining anything, she was salvaging. Salvaging her pride. ''He has very strong feelings about the
age difference between us. If I tell him about the
baby and he proposes, I know it's only because he
feels it's the honorable thing to do—''

The laugh that escaped Shelby's lips had no mirth
to it. ''Well, it is.''

''I don't want honorable, I want love.''

''Then give him a chance to give it to you.''

''And if he doesn't?'' Lacy asked. ''What do I do
with my heart then, Shelby? How do I put together
all the pieces then if I see him just going through the
motions and not meaning it?'' She couldn't do that
to herself or to him. Certainly not to Chase and the
baby who was to come. ''No, it's better my way. I
won't be making a fool of myself and I'll still have
my pride.'' Picking up Chase, Lacy rose. ''Thanks.''

Shelby looked at her incredulously. ''For what?''

''For letting me talk to you.''

''If I had talked you into doing the right thing,
then you could thank me.'' She hadn't done anything
helpful. She rose and gave Lacy a hug. ''Let me
know where you decide to go.''

Lacy nodded and crossed to the door. ''As soon
as I figure it out myself.''

Shelby stood very still as she looked through the

window and watched Lacy make her way down the block. Closing her eyes, she shook her head, then began to count to fifty.

She got to twenty-nine before she ran out of patience. Shelby turned on her heel and headed for the phone in the storeroom.

CHAPTER FIFTEEN

LEANING LOW over his horse, Connor pressed his knees against the stallion's flanks, urging the animal on.

A single refrain beat in his brain. *I need to get there in time.*

Things had finally begun to take on a definite shape in his life, a good shape. He had a new ranch, a new family, not to mention a new son, all of which provided him with a new purpose in life.

And he was in love with a beautiful, selfless woman and he was going to do his damnedest to keep her in his life no matter what it took.

He'd made up his mind about it today, while he'd been riding the range, checking the new stock he'd bought at the auction. He thought more clearly in the open, away from distractions. Despite the concessions he'd made, willingly and otherwise, toward being a businessman and living a breath away from the twenty-first century, he was still an old-fashioned sort of man. He needed open spaces to clear his head. And to examine his heart.

There was a time Connor would have said he

didn't have to bother with his heart, but that was far in the past. He knew he'd been wrong. The heart was the most important organ. Without it, the brain was just keeping a shell alive.

He was tired of being a shell. He wanted to be a flesh and blood man. More important, he wanted to be the man who made love to Lacy every night.

Just when it appeared everything was finally going right and he'd finally come to his senses and was on the right track, he'd been suckered with a one-two punch when he wasn't looking. At least it sure felt that way.

The cell phone he'd purchased at the behest of his foreman, and which he'd been secretly convinced would never ring, had rung. Thinking it was Lacy, he'd been surprised to hear his mother's voice on the line. Megan had sounded so serious when she'd returned his greeting that Connor had instantly known something was wrong.

And was it ever. Very wrong. Not one something but two. And Connor had been completely unprepared for either of them.

Megan had begun with no preamble, no small talk. "Connor, Janelle's escaped."

It sounded too fantastic to be true. "Escaped? How? When?" The last he had heard, the woman was in the Austin jail awaiting trial.

His mother spared him any dramatic pauses, giving him the basics.

"It seems a woman claiming to be her lawyer came to see her. And since she was Janelle's lawyer, she was able to see Janelle in a sequestered room." Megan sighed. "Which was her mistake."

"What do you mean?"

"The official story is that the woman told the guard she was ready to leave, and after she did, the guard discovered it was Janelle who had been allowed to walk out. Apparently the two women look enough alike to pass for each other."

"So then the woman helped her escape?"

"No, Janelle knocked her out. Jake said Janelle positioned the woman so she was sitting in a chair with her back to the door. The guard thought nothing of it when he let Janelle out."

Frustrated anger had filled his mother's voice. He knew what she was thinking. The same thing he was. Just when they all thought they were finally rid of the woman, Janelle had found a way to pose another threat.

"She is resourceful, I'll give her that, Connor."

Resourceful was one way to put it. It wouldn't have been his choice of words. "Only because you're a lady, Mother," he'd commented. "So I take it she's still on the loose?"

"I'm afraid so. The police are out looking for her right now, along with Jake and Max. I don't think Lacy or you are in any immediate danger, but, Connor..." This time, she had paused. "I'm afraid there's more."

Connor braced himself, but it hadn't been nearly enough. "What?"

"Shelby just called me from the diner. Lacy's leaving with Chase."

He'd almost dropped the cell phone. "Leaving?" He'd echoed the word in disbelief, its hard edges scraping over him. "Leaving where?"

"She's leaving Austin. And, Connor—"

A sense of urgency seized him. There was no time to waste. "I'll talk to you later, Mother. And thanks for letting me know." He'd cut off the connection even though she was saying something. Probably wishing him luck.

He was going to need more than luck, but it was a start.

All the way to the ranch house, Connor searched his mind for what he'd say to her. Nothing seemed right. He vacillated between ordering Lacy to stay and begging her to stay.

And letting her go.

He knew the last was the only right thing, the honorable thing to do. To let her go so she could move on with her life. After all, it wasn't as if he hadn't known this day was coming, hadn't tried to prepare himself for it by keeping her at arm's length. But he had failed miserably. And now that the day was here, the only thing he wanted to do was postpone it. Indefinitely.

Arriving at the house, Connor jumped off his horse, leaving it in the care of one of the ranch hands.

"You going out again?" the man called after him, but Connor didn't hear him. He was too focused on finding Lacy. On praying he wasn't too late.

The second he walked in, he knew what his mother had said was true. Lacy was leaving. The two suitcases lined up by the door bore silent testimony.

He could have sworn the very air felt different somehow. Stifling, oppressive.

Damn it, she wasn't leaving. Not without one hell of a convincing argument.

Like a man possessed, Connor ran through the house searching for her, bellowing her name at the top of his lungs.

He found her in the nursery, packing Chase's things. The baby was in his crib, sound asleep. Oblivious to the upheaval that was about to occur in his life.

When Lacy turned to look at him, he saw that she'd been crying. Some of the rage within him abated, mitigated by the sight of her damp cheeks.

But he was still angry.

Hands framing the doorway on either side, he physically barred her exit. "What the hell do you think you're doing?"

Somehow, despite the fury she saw in his eyes,

she managed to find her tongue. "What are you do-ing here? You were supposed to be gone all day."

"Sorry to disappoint you," He bit off the words. For a moment, his eyes shifted to the baby's crib to reassure himself that Chase was still there. "Lucky thing I invested in this little doo-hickey." He held up the cell phone. "Otherwise, my mother couldn't have called me." His eyes narrowed as he struggled to curb the rising tide of fury. "She said Shelby called to tell her what you were going to do." His face hardened. "Seems you can tell everyone else but me what you're planning."

She banked down the hurt at the sarcasm in his voice. Maybe he was entitled to it. She didn't know. All she knew was that this was hard enough to do without being confronted by him.

"All right." Lacy raised her chin and delivered the message he'd demanded. "I'm leaving. Satis-fied?"

He threw the cell phone across the room. It landed on the floor just shy of the wall. "Just like that? Without a word?"

She picked up a long white envelope from the bed and held it out to him. "I wrote you this letter."

He knocked the envelope aside. Did she think he was some damn employee she was giving a sever-ance note to? "I don't care about a damn letter." He loomed over her. "I want you to tell me, Lacy. Face to face. I want you to tell me why you're sneaking off like some thief in the night.''

Lacy stood her ground, refusing to be intimidated. ''I'm not sneaking off.''

''Damn straight you're not.'' Not if he had anything to say about it.

She sighed, her courage flagging dangerously. Nothing seemed to make sense anymore. ''I just thought it would be better this way.''

His eyes widened incredulously. ''Better for who? For you?''

She'd thought it over a hundred times since she'd made up her mind, jumping from one side to the other and back again. If it wasn't for the baby she was carrying, she would have stayed, even if staying meant dying slowly by inches because she couldn't have him.

But the coming baby changed everything. She couldn't add this to the weight he was already carrying. ''No, for you.''

Connor's mouth dropped open. Was she serious? ''How?'' he demanded. ''How is it better for me to come home and find that you and Chase are gone? That the woman who's brought sunshine into my world is gone?''

It took a second for her to peel away the anger wrapped around his words and absorb their meaning. When she did, she was stunned, certain she hadn't heard correctly.

"What?"

"You heard me." What did she want, diagrams? All right, he'd give her diagrams. "I said you brought sunshine into my world. Colors, lights." He fairly shouted the words into her face. Getting hold of himself, he lowered his voice. "You made me feel like a man again, Lacy, and maybe I don't have the right to make you stay, but I'm going to try anyway."

It was as if her brain had gone numb. "Wait, I don't understand."

"Then I'll say it more simply." His eyes held hers, making his plea far more eloquently than he could. "Don't go. Please."

She wanted to melt into his arms, to say yes, she'd stay. Stay forever and always.

But she couldn't stay, not for the wrong reasons.

She felt shaky inside as she tried to sort his words out. "Listen, if you're saying that because you feel guilty—"

Now it was his turn to be confused. "Guilty about what?"

Exasperated, she dragged her hand through her hair. "Maybe guilty's the wrong word." She turned to face him. "Responsible," she decided. "If you're saying this because you feel responsible for some reason, don't. It's not your fault, it's mine."

Her words were only making things murkier. "What isn't your fault? Lacy, I haven't got a clue what you're talking about or why you're leaving like this, and I'm not going to read any damn letter to find out." He caught her shoulders, afraid she might run out on him. "What are you talking about and what the hell am I supposed to feel guilty about?"

"Responsible," she corrected.

"Whatever," he snapped, in no mood for semantics. "Don't you realize that the only thing I feel is love? Love for you, love for Chase."

She couldn't get herself to believe what he was saying. This was a dream she was having. The dream she was always having. "And the baby?"

"I already said Chase," he told her impatiently.

"No, not Chase." Tremors began to shake the castle in the clouds he'd begun forming for her as it dawned on her. "You don't know, do you?"

He felt more tired than he had in a long while. "Apparently I know very little about what's going on." And then it hit him. Suddenly. Like a ton of bricks. Hit him so hard that for a second, the very breath was knocked out of him. "You're pregnant, aren't you?" It all made sense now. The pale color, the tired appearance, her refusal to see Abby. Everything. It all tied together.

"Yes, but—"

"But?" he echoed, catching her hands. "There is no but. You're pregnant and the baby's mine. And Chase is mine," he informed her sharply. And then his tone softened. "The only thing that isn't mine is you. I guess I did too good a job convincing you that I was too old for you.''

"Too old?" She stared at him. "Is that why you think I'm going?"

He couldn't think of any other reason. "Well, isn't it?"

She didn't know whether to laugh or cry and did a little of both. "I'm going because I don't want you to feel you have to marry me out of a sense of obligation. I don't want to hear another proposal from you, because this time I might not have the strength of character to turn you down."

He drew her to him, not firmly but gently. Hopefully. "Then don't turn me down. Say yes, Lacy. Say yes and accept my love."

Her heart began to hammer. She refused to listen to what her heart was saying, knowing how easily it could seduce her into believing dreams. "You're just saying that."

"Yes, I am saying that. But give me a chance and I'll prove it to you, Lacy. Every day for the rest of your life." He took her hands in his again. "Lacy, I'm not the sharpest tack on the board. Sometimes it takes me a while to work things through, to see them in their true light. But I've worked it through now, and I know that I'd be the luckiest man under the sun having you for a wife, even for a little while."

It finally penetrated. She finally allowed herself to believe. He wanted her. Connor really wanted her.

She felt as if she was going to cry again. But this time, her tears would be tears of happiness. "Why only a little while? Are you planning to make this a five-year renewable marriage?"

His mouth curved, but his smile was sad. "No, because I *am* too old for you. They say that men reach their peak at nineteen."

She didn't care what they said. "That's just an average, and there is nothing average about you, Connor O'Hara. There never has been." She threaded her arms around his waist. "I know that firsthand."

Having her against him like this felt so right. "So is that a yes?"

She turned her face to his. "It's always been yes, Connor, right from the very start. You were just too stubborn to hear."

"I plan to rectify that, starting now."

She felt the smile spreading throughout her whole body. She hugged him harder. "Just what did you have in mind?"

Connor brought his face to hers, his eyes making love to her. "I'm a man of few words, Lacy, and I've already used them all up today. I'd rather show you."

And he did.

EPILOGUE

WEAVING a path through the sea of friends and relatives who had gathered to celebrate his son's first birthday, Connor made his way to Lacy.

His wife.

It was still hard to believe, but then, it had only been a little over a week since they'd gotten married, postponing their honeymoon until after Chase's birthday party. He figured he'd get used to it in about another hundred years or so.

Nodding at his mother, he maneuvered between Max and Chelsea. Lacy had just turned from Jake and Camille after offering them a tray full of hors d'oeuvres.

Connor whispered in her ear. "You're doing too much again."

Lacy smiled at his concern. It was rather nice being looked after, even if she wasn't used to it. "I feel fine, Connor."

He raised a skeptical brow. "You wouldn't admit it if you weren't."

She laughed. He was beginning to know her. Finally. "Okay, you've got me there, but I really am feeling fine.'' In fact, if she felt any better, it might very well be illegal. Despite the fact that Janelle was still out there somewhere, posing a possible threat to her, Lacy had never felt better in her whole life.

She paused to rest one hand against Connor's chest as she looked into his eyes. ''Trust me.''

He took the opportunity to brush a kiss against her lips. ''With my life.''

''Hey, you two, break it up or we'll have to turn a hose on you,'' Lana Lord warned good-naturedly. ''Just because you're newlyweds doesn't mean you have to rub it in for the rest of us. Some of us are still looking for our one true love.''

''You'd have to stop working for that to happen,'' Lacy told her. It was a known fact that Lana devoted every waking moment to building up her business, a specialty shop for babies.

''Yes, well, maybe someday,'' Lana allowed. ''Speaking of working, I'm afraid I'm going to have to run right after Chase blows out his candle.''

''The inventory can wait, Lana,'' her brother Garrett told her.

''I'll have you know it isn't inventory, it's some befuddled new father I promised to help. He wants me to demystify fatherhood for him.''

Connor laughed, looking toward Chase. The little boy was enjoying a rousing game of patty-cake with his grandmother. ''Lots of luck.''

''Here.'' Determined, Abby took the tray from

Lacy, her tone telling her new sister-in-law that she would brook no protest. "Let me take that from you. You've got enough to handle."

Surrendering the tray, Lacy looked at Connor. "Did you tell her?"

About to make the rest of the rounds, Abby stopped. She looked from Connor to Lacy. "Tell me what?"

"No." Connor answered Lacy, aware that they were attracting more than just Abby's attention. "But I guess this is as good a time as any to make the announcement."

"Tell me what?" Abby repeated as her husband, Kyle, joined her. "What announcement?" she asked when neither Connor nor Lacy answered.

Lacy raised her voice, though from the looks of those around her, it wasn't necessary. Everyone was listening. "That there's going to be another place setting at the table next Easter." Her smile deepened as she felt Connor slip his arm around her.

The next moment, they were submerged in well-wishers. Jake elbowed his way to the center of the crowd. He stared at Lacy. "You're...?"

She was beaming. "Yes."

"Wow." Jake turned to Connor. "Well, you certainly don't waste time once you put your mind to something, do you?"

"Hey, I'm an old man," Connor said, deadpan,

though his eyes gave him away. "I don't have time to procrastinate."

"Yeah, he took care of the baby making up front," Lacy teased, twining her arms around his waist as she looked around her, basking in the attention of the family she had always wanted.

Singing "Happy Birthday" to the little boy who had won all their hearts was temporarily postponed and hearty congratulations were issued as the Maitlands prepared to expand their ranks yet again.

And happily so.